First published August 2020

www.peterboonauthor.com

Cover design by info@amapopico.com and Book Cover Zone.

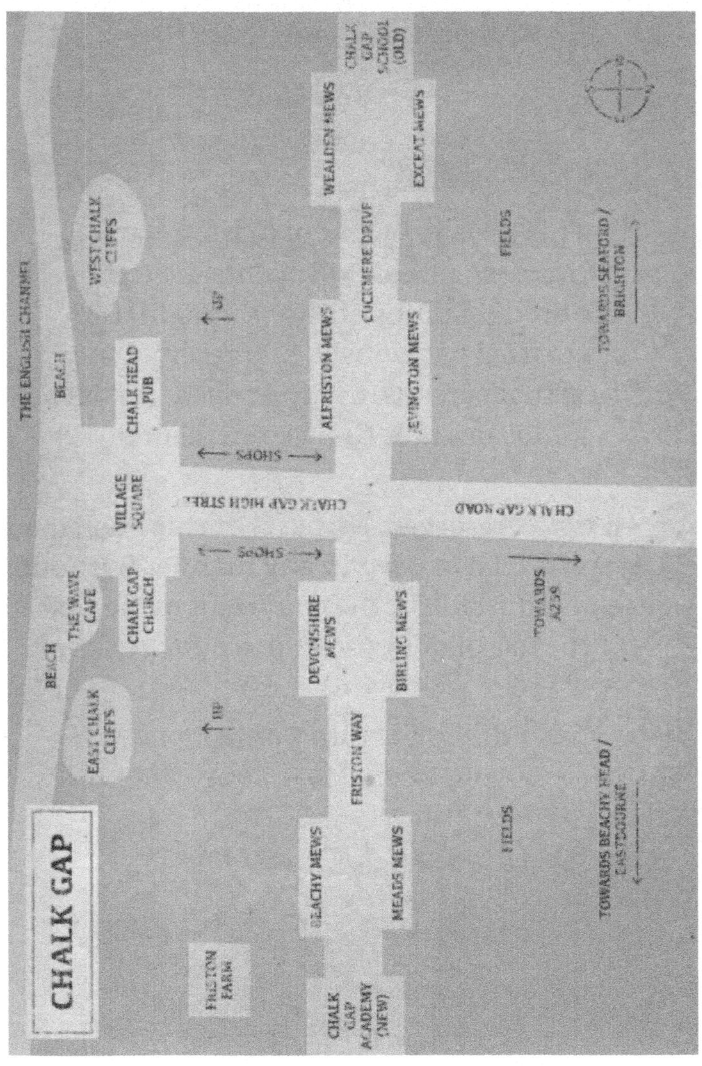
CHALK GAP
THE ENGLISH CHANNEL
BEACH
WEST CHALK CLIFFS
EAST CHALK CLIFFS
BEACH
THE WAVE CAFE
CHALK GAP CHURCH
VILLAGE SQUARE
CHALK HEAD PUB
SHOPS
SHOPS
CHALK GAP HIGH STRE
CHALK GAP ROAD
FRISTON FARM
CHALK GAP ACADEMY (NEW)
BEACHY MEWS
MEADS MEWS
FRISTON WAY
DEVONSHIRE MEWS
BIRLING MEWS
ALFRISTON MEWS
JEVINGTON MEWS
CUCKMERE DRIVE
WEALDEN MEWS
EXCEAT MEWS
CHALK GAP SCHOOL (OLD)
FIELDS
FIELDS
TOWARDS A259
TOWARDS BEACHY HEAD / EASTBOURNE
TOWARDS SEAFORD / BRIGHTON

1

Eastbourne, just a few miles from our village, is officially the sunniest place in the UK. Whoever made this assessment hadn't met our Head Teacher, Miss Finch, who lived there.

This thought occurred to me at the back of the school hall as I watched my colleagues – experienced professionals - scuttle about in terror as Miss Finch summoned them. I wanted a word with our Deputy Head but it wasn't a good time to interrupt.

'Ladies and gentlemen... get over here now!' Finch bellowed from the height of the stage, which allowed her to tower over everyone in the room despite her tiny five foot stature. A deliberate choice for certain. She also didn't seem to care that the rudeness of her barked command cancelled out the politeness of the term used to address them.

A spotlight shone on her in the dim hall, as if she was the only glimpse of light in the darkness - when in fact the opposite was true.

'Ladies and gentlemen,' she repeated. 'In less than 24 hours, I am meant to be on this stage telling all the inhabitants of *your* simple tiny village how the new Chalk Gap Academy will shape the future of all of its young people.'

She pushed her glasses down her nose and peered down. The movement made me conscious of my own glasses and I nudged them up onto my face.

From my viewpoint out of sight at the back of the room, the set-up for tomorrow's launch day didn't seem to be going well. And yes, I said launch day. I know, it sounds more like a Black Friday sale than a school reopening. The academy chain who took us over has corporate terms for everything.

'Although its predecessor hardly did any favours for the current generation. If you cannot get a simple technical run-through of my speech right, no wonder you seem to have trouble running a school.'

'Anne, I don't think that's -' our Deputy Head and one of my two housemates, Kat Parker, said.

'It is Miss Finch!' she boomed. 'Miss Parker, you must address me as Miss Finch.'

Even though Kat had her back to me, I could imagine her rolling her eyes. There were no children around, so it should have been perfectly normal to use first names. But she didn't allow it in front of *junior* colleagues, and she was definitely

Miss Finch through and through. She probably came out of her mother's womb as Miss Finch, giving feedback on how the birthing experience requires improvement.

'Miss Finch,' Kat said as she let out a sigh. 'I don't think that's very fair -'

'You don't think, Miss Parker? You don't think?' I could tell she was enjoying this pantomime at Kat's expense. 'That's the trouble – you don't think. Surely if you had any thoughts worth having, you'd be the one up on this stage, not me.'

I saw Kat's head bow. That one would sting - she'd applied for the Head Teacher's job herself and not even made it to interview. But Miss Finch had moved her attention to our caretaker, Carol Fletcher, who was operating the stage lighting from a desk in the centre of the hall.

'For crying out loud, Mrs Fletcher, will you please keep the spotlight on me while I address the group?'

The spotlight vibrated suddenly from left to right, plunging her in and out of the light, as if it was shaking its head in defiance.

'Unless you want to join Mr Fletcher at home to enjoy your retirement *together*?' The spotlight became perfectly still. Carol's husband Brian was our Head of Maths and had been at the school for over 30 years – until Miss Finch arrived. Within two weeks we received an email from Dylan, Miss

Finch's PA, that Brian and the school had mutually agreed his early retirement.

Dylan Spence was one of the few silver linings from the new academy. As I thought about him, I noticed him turn round and blow a theatrical kiss at Carol to cheer her up. The spotlight wobbled again as I saw her shoulders shake from laughter, but luckily Miss Finch was engaged elsewhere.

'Miss Finch,' Kat started pointedly. 'We're all giving up time in our summer break to help the school. You don't need to threaten anyone.' This was why I admired Kat. She stayed quiet after her own humiliation but wouldn't allow Finch to embarrass anyone else.

'Oh, don't I?' Miss Finch replied in mock innocence. 'Okay then, Miss Parker. I give in. You can clearly do better than me. Mrs Fletcher, put the spotlight on Miss Parker please.'

The spotlight swayed once more in obvious uncertainty at this unusual command. Finch spoke again with deliberate emphasis on each word. 'I said – put the spotlight on Miss Parker. Now.'

I watched helplessly as the light moved from Miss Finch to my friend. 'There we go, Miss Parker. You have all the attention you want. The floor is yours. Let's see how you do.'

Kat stared up at Finch. She shook her head and stepped out of the spotlight. As the light shone back on our Head Teacher and she continued with her monologue, I heard a voice behind me.

'Miss Finch would make a perfect murder victim.'

I turned round to see Noah Oxley. Noah is my student library assistant and fellow fan of murder mystery novels.

'Ssshhh!' I hissed in panicked tones as I waved him outside. 'Come and speak to me out here.'

I couldn't let Miss Finch see him; to say she didn't 'get' Noah was an understatement. Most people find him very endearing. In fact, the school has gained high praise locally for the way he's at the heart of our activities. It gives lots of anxious parents hope that their own child's needs will be very well looked after.

But Finch didn't agree. As soon as she saw him help at an open evening, she immediately insisted 'that boy' be put out of sight, and had tried to keep him there ever since. I'd even heard she'd tried to stop him continuing on with us to do his A Levels in September. Rather than hold any grudge against Finch for this treatment, he'd cast her as a hated potential murder victim.

'Think about it, Sir – it's a great murder mystery plot. Who killed the hated Head Teacher? Everyone is a suspect. Everyone has a motive. Only Edward Crisp, school librarian, and Noah Oakley, his brilliant teenage assistant, can solve the case.'

'Firstly, it's still *Mr* Crisp to you. And don't say things like that.' I looked back through the doorway and changed to a whisper. 'She wouldn't be thrilled if she heard you killing her off.'

'Oh, come on, Sir, this is fate. We both love murder mysteries and now we'll get to solve our own real life one.'

It's true, I've loved murder mysteries as long as I can remember. The Famous Five and the Secret Seven were my first love – groups of kids all banding together to solve a crime and right a wrong. As I got a little older, I moved on to Agatha Christie's Hercule Poirot and Miss Marple; I became obsessed with them.

Since Noah started helping me in the library, it's the main thing we have in common. I think the logical structure and order of murder mysteries appeals to us both. Good and evil, right and wrong, innocent and guilty. It helps us find our place in the world.

But for Noah, I worry it goes even further. I think he believes we've been brought together like Poirot and Hastings, Holmes and Watson - a crime-solving duo who will put the world to rights.

'You said it yourself, Noah. This is real life. No one will murder Miss Finch, and we will not have a mystery to solve.'

Imagine my surprise the next day when everything he said came true.

2

I never thought that conversation with Noah would lead to me writing this – a first-person account of a genuine murder mystery. And don't worry, this isn't one where it turns out the narrator did it.

I just wanted to have an accurate record of everything that happened. And my doctor keeps telling me to keep a mood diary – I guess this is close enough. That means you – the imaginary 'you' as I doubt anyone will ever see this, or any of my work – can be my reader.

Before I get back to the story, I should say a little about where we live. Chalk Gap is a tiny seaside village in East Sussex, just outside of Eastbourne. We are just past the famous Beachy Head, nestled between two beautiful chalk cliffs of our own.

Yes, a tiny seaside village. If you're playing along with Noah's theory then, I suppose it is the kind of place you might expect to find a murder mystery – a kind of *Miss Marple* meets *Broadchurch*.

Otherwise, we are just a typical coastal town.

I won't say everyone knows absolutely everyone, because real life isn't like that, but you get the idea. I've lived here all of my adult life, as have most people in Chalk Gap.

My family owns the one pub we have here, the Chalk Inn. It overlooks the beach on the West Chalk side of the village square where the two cliffs drop to meet the seafront and the foot of our high street. My Dad always says, 'if you hit water you've gone too far,' and then waits for the laugh that never comes.

With the scene set a little, I'll go back to Noah and his prediction of Miss Finch's murder. It's hard to describe Noah Oxley when you haven't met him. The first thing you'll notice is the way he speaks, which has one setting: loud, fast and over-excited.

Then you'll notice his appearance: unkempt, unbrushed hair, along with unmatched, odd looking clothes that don't quite fit. He might proudly tell you that his mum lets him shop for himself.

Next you smell him – he hasn't quite grasped the difference between antiperspirant and body spray, and this often means you are greeted with a heady mix of sweat and African musk if he stands too close to you (which he often does).

But he has a brilliant mind, is a great student librarian and someone I get on very well with. I tried to remember this as I hustled him into the library, out of the way of Miss Finch.

'Sir, I came to help!' he said proudly as I looked over my shoulder in terror. 'Mrs Fletcher was in my mum's café this morning and she told me you were getting ready for tomorrow. I had to finish helping Mum first, but then she dropped me off so I could get here ASAP.'

Like me, Carol would be very stressed today. I'd already seen what she had to endure just operating the lighting deck. Poor woman. She probably just wanted to eat her breakfast in peace and wouldn't be prepared for a full interrogation from Noah.

Unlike me, she didn't have Noah in the middle of her room as Miss Finch approached. He was excitedly talking about all the things he could help with when I heard the all too familiar clip clop of her shoes coming closer. They sounded heavier and angrier than usual, if that was possible. Though it might have been the shiny flooring in her ridiculously expensive new school building.

Miss Finch was five feet tall at the very most, but whoever said 'good things come in small packages' hadn't met her. She was always immaculately dressed with some sense of style for a lady in her fifties – short elfin hair and bright, colour co-ordinated outfits with a suit, shoes and earrings that always matched. This was accompanied by a false, business-like smile which seemed as carefully chosen as her clothes - the difference being it would disappear at a moment's notice.

So you can see why I didn't want to be on the wrong side of her by having Noah in the library against her explicit instructions. I quickly persuaded him to hide at the last minute, which is no minor feat for a sixteen-year-old with Asperger's.

Miss Finch marched in and surveyed the room with narrowed, suspicious eyes.

'That boy, Mr Crisp. Is he here?'

She spoke slowly and menacingly. The fake smile wasn't even there.

'Which boy, Miss Finch? Noah? No, I haven't seen him. I don't think he's due in today, is he?'

I garbled the words out as quickly as I could, forgetting to breathe as I said them. I am no good at lying or last-minute situations; my heart felt like it would explode through my chest.

'He's here, in my school building, he's here, I know he is! So where is he? I was clear that there should be no student helpers today. And especially not that boy! He will ruin everything.'

I looked at Miss Finch as her anger erupted. Her face was bright red and her voice had become a high-pitch squeal. Now this was unusual. I knew that she had strong views on Noah's presence at the launch event, so I expected her to check he wasn't around. But her particular brand of malice was usually calm, cold and carefully delivered, like a poisonous snake biting its victim. This was different. Miss Finch was rattled, and I didn't know why.

Not knowing what to say, I allowed a silence to pass as she seemed to realise that she had shown a rare moment of weakness. As she regained her composure, I saw the familiar false smile appear on her face. She was about to get her power back.

'Mr Crisp, you've been the librarian here for nine years, haven't you?'

She didn't wait for me to answer as she glanced around the new school library, the library I'd had sleepless nights over for weeks. Any sudden change of circumstance is agony for me, and I'd put my heart and soul into getting the new library layout right. I knew I'd done a good job, but Miss Finch had other ideas.

'Then I know I need not tell you the standard that the new library needs to be at for tomorrow's launch day. A librarian who doesn't have his library up to scratch for such an important public event wouldn't be in employment for another nine days, let alone nine years. I trust this is a work in progress.'

With that parting shot delivered, she marched out.

3

I was trying to work out exactly what had just happened with Miss Finch when Noah reappeared out of the stock cupboard. It worried me he'd heard what she'd said and would be upset. I didn't even have time to ask him as another visitor joined us.

'Are you two weirdos plotting your next murder?'

'You know you can't speak to me like that, Gracie. And please don't speak to Noah like that either.'

Gracie is the daughter of Tim Hunt, our Chair of Governors, who my mum always referred to as 'that flash b word in the Mercedes.' That's not me censoring Mum, she actually says 'b word.' Tim was the driving force behind the academy takeover and seems to run our school from the passenger seat. Which is probably why Gracie spoke to me in the way she did without caring.

'Ooh and don't speak to Noah like that either,' she mimicked as she scrolled through her phone, not even bothering to look at me as she insulted me. 'You mean the same Noah who you just told Miss Finch isn't here?'

'I was here, I was just hiding in the cupboard,' Noah said, somewhat unhelpfully.

'My dad saw you arrive anyway,' she announced, rolling her eyes. 'Mr Crisp, you know he isn't supposed to be here.'

So that was it – the reason Miss Finch was so unusually flustered a few minutes before. Tim must have spotted Noah and tackled her about it. She would not have appreciated being made to look stupid in front of the Chair of Governors. He probably shared the same Draconian views about Noah that Miss Finch did. His daughter certainly did.

'You know it's because they think you're a weirdo, don't you?' This time she directed her comment at Noah, though she still barely bothered to look at him. 'They think you will be a serial killer.'

'That's enough, Gracie -' I tried to interrupt.

'They don't want everyone coming to the launch day tomorrow and thinking we're some kind of charity for freaks.'

'Gracie, I said -'

'Everyone in Chalk Gap thinks it anyway,' she said as she typed on her phone. I saw her screen shine at me with the sharp blue and white light of her social media page. She raised her eyes from her device to focus on Noah with a smirk. 'Someone even told me that your mum serves up your victims in her burgers at the café.'

'Enough, Gracie -'

'It's alright Sir, I told them not to say that... If they don't want to end up as his next victim.'

'Gracie, I said ENOUGH!' I shouted and surprised myself.

'It's okay, Sir,' Noah spoke up. He looked her straight in the eye and calmly continued. 'Gracie, thank you for letting me know. But please tell everyone I can't possibly be a psycho killer. If I was, there's no way you'd still be alive.'

Gracie looked stunned, and Noah wore a triumphant smile.

'Wait till I tell my dad you just made a death threat to me. And that he stood by and let you,' she said, glaring at me. 'Let's see what happens then!' With that, she flounced out.

There was silence for a moment. Neither of us were used to real life confrontation. Our little corner of the world – the library, shelves of books, murder mysteries – usually shielded us from it. Or so I hoped.

'Well done for standing up to her, Noah.'

'It's okay, Sir. My mum says that some people just need putting in their place.'

That's the kind of thing my mum always says to me too. I think protective mothers must be part of the package with social difficulties. Although Noah seemed to deal with it better than I could, I was still worried about Gracie's treatment of him.

'I need to ask you, does Gracie say that kind of thing a lot to you? Because it seems like she does.'

Noah thought carefully for a moment and then spoke.

'I suppose she does, but it doesn't bother me.'

'Are you sure?' I asked.

'Well, it bothers me a little.'

Hearing him say that affected me. I saw a lot of myself in Noah, though he seemed to have a tenacity that I didn't have. Or he was just oblivious to most things while I was a bag of anxiety. I was bullied in school, badly, and there was one prime culprit, like Gracie, who just seemed to have it in for me because I was different. Thinking of that spurred me on.

'We can do something about it, Noah, if you want to.'

'I don't know really. I don't think there's much point to be honest, and now I've stood up to her, I don't think she'll say it anymore.'

Poor Noah. He really did not understand how people like Gracie work.

'One thing though, Mr Crisp. If Miss Finch told you I wasn't allowed in to help with the launch day, you should have told her she was wrong.'

I would have given anything to think as simplistically about things as he did.

'It doesn't work like that. She's my boss.'

'That doesn't matter, Sir. She was wrong and you should have told her.' I could feel his intense gaze on me as he spoke. 'You said I stood up to Gracie, but you didn't do the same with Miss Finch. Now the launch day won't be as good because I'm great at helping, and I feel sad that I won't be a part of it.'

I knew what I had to do.

4

Miss Finch's 'leadership suite' represented everything that was wrong with the new school. The ridiculous name for starters. Our old Head Teacher, lovely Terry Eldridge, had his old office in the main school corridor - a fairly small room shared with his secretary Brenda, but with a meeting room at the back if he needed privacy.

Staff and students were welcome in there anytime; the door was literally always open, with a wooden wedge that students used to steal but get caught in the act by Brenda. Terry and Brenda's respective grandchildren looked out at you joyfully from photo frames on their desks. The office was always a mess, but it guaranteed you a big smile, a cup of tea from Brenda and a sherbet lemon from Terry's top drawer.

In contrast, the leadership suite was a large corporate space which didn't seem to belong in a school. It could have been an executive office in a bank or an IT company. We had to swipe our newly issued ID cards even to gain access to the 'welcome area' (and I use that term loosely).

Once you were in, you would see a large open space with one desk strangely placed in the very centre for Miss Finch's Personal Assistant. The four offices in each corner of the room were glass from floor to ceiling, so you could see everything in there, if you dared to look. Everything you could see was brand new and brilliant white, but the shiny sparkling furniture couldn't make up for the place having no heart.

The largest belonged to Miss Finch, with a white, plain desk in the corner (empty save her computer on it), facing away so she had her back to the glass. The only other furniture in the room was a meeting table with six chairs. The next biggest office was Tim Hunt's, with a similar setup on a smaller scale. No photos of Gracie in sight. Then there was a 'hot desk' office for academy chain staff or other governors to use when visiting. I noticed that all three offices had water dispensers, complete with single-use plastic cups. Typically corporate and certainly not environmentally friendly.

Finally, the smallest office by far (almost an afterthought in the furthest corner of the suite) belonged to our existing Deputy Head, Kat Parker.

Kat's office was the only one reminiscent of the offices in the old building. There were flowers on her desk, a crowded bookcase behind it and a photo of her and her mum blu tacked to the wall. It didn't fit with the rest of the 'suite'. I felt that Kat wouldn't be occupying the office for long if Miss Finch had her way.

As I arrived to speak to Miss Finch, Dylan Spence, her P.A., was on the phone but smiled and waved to acknowledge me.

'Oh yes, I completely understand, Mrs Ellison… Well, we can't have that can we?... Okay, so one option is for you to put it in writing to discuss at our next Governor's meeting on the 28th… I must say though, my grandma is over in Eastbourne right next to one school… No, she doesn't have any trouble at all, she says they're delightful!'

He winked at me as he listened patiently to the other end of the conversation.

'… yes, most of our students here are lovely… you see some of them at church on Sundays?... oh that's wonderful, I go to church every Sunday too… oh yes, strict Catholics, all of my family…'

There was a long pause as he was obviously letting the lonely old lady speak. He'd been Miss Finch's P.A. at her last school, and she insisted he came with her. Poor Brenda was relegated to the post room and the photocopier before deciding to join Terry in early retirement. But Dylan was nothing like Miss Finch. He was human.

'Oh yes, she loves living there... she has them all running errands to the shop for her after school... yes, it makes a difference when you're trying to enjoy your retirement doesn't it?... Okay,

Mrs Ellison, so would you like me to pop it on the next meeting agenda?... you don't want to take it any further, oh that's wonderful!... yes I'll tell my grandma all about you next time I speak to her... and don't you forget, my name is Dylan Spence, and you can call me directly any time... oh thank you, you're very kind... you take care Mrs Ellison, goodbye!'

He put the phone down and smiled at me.

'Sorry about that, Edward, another old dear down the street concerned about the school moving to this side of the village.'

'Don't worry. I didn't know you had a grandma in Eastbourne. I thought you weren't from this area?'

'Oh, I don't, I just made that up to calm her down,' he replied. 'Both of my grandmas died when I was young.'

There was nothing wrong with a white lie to pacify an old lady – was there? Dylan had made lots of effort with everyone since arriving: bringing cakes in, organising staff drinks, keeping everyone up to date with the gossip on Miss Finch. He had made it clear that he was definitely on the staff's side. But after the conversation I'd just seen, how much of it was genuine?

'Anyway Edward, my fine friend, what can I do for you today?'

I explained I wanted to see Miss Finch about something important but he gestured towards her office, where she was sat at her desk listening to Tim, who was sat casually perched on her meeting table, legs swinging and coffee in hand, like he owned the place.

'Tim told me not to disturb them until the staff meeting. Sorry, Edward.'

I didn't know what to do. As I told you, I hated confrontation, but I had worked up the courage to go up there and speak to Miss Finch about the possible bullying issue. I'd made it there, but I hadn't really thought of what I'd do if she wasn't around. I mumbled something about trying to speak to her later when I heard a voice behind me.

'Will I do as a second choice?'

I turned round to see Kat Parker smiling at me. Her smile was always genuine, but I noticed the bags under her eyes, the coffee stain on her white shirt and her usual beautiful afro hairstyle tied back tightly in a hurry. I'd noticed a lot lately how stressed and tired Kat was. We shared a house together with our other friend and colleague Patrick, and Kat's summers were usually three weeks abroad followed by another three relaxing with us – back garden barbecues, beach days and *Netflix* marathons.

But she'd spent the entire summer in the confines of this 'leadership suite' getting the school ready for the academy reopening. She was around the same age as me and Patrick, but made Deputy Head in the first five years of her career before she was even 30. She just didn't seem to fit into this false, corporate world that school management had turned into.

'Come into my office, Ed, and have a catch-up. I haven't even had a visitor in there yet.'

Kat is the only person who gets away with calling me Ed, I usually hate it. 'A catch-up? We live together.'

'I know, but a work catch-up. Besides, you don't like hot drinks, so it gives me an excuse to use the water dispenser I'm not meant to use.' She laughed as she headed into the hot desk office.

'Don't get caught!' Dylan shouted to her as she passed him.

I headed into her office and immediately started admiring her bookcase. It's a habit of mine anywhere I go to look at people's book collection – it can tell you so much about them. I noted several books on school management and student behaviour, women in leadership, various books on human behaviour and the recently acclaimed *Why I'm No Longer Talking To White People About Race*, though I knew Kat's dog-eared copy was at least a couple of years old. These non-fiction texts were littered amongst female written classics such as *Jane Eyre*, *Pride and Prejudice*, *Wuthering Heights*,

Wide Sargasso Sea, *The Colour Purple* and others.

'I'm still forced to keep all my favourite books here seeing as I can't get near the bookcases at home,' she joked as she returned with two cups of water. My book collections were the source of multiple (mostly) jokey arguments at home; they'd long since over-spilled from the shelves and were even in little piles around the house.

'So, how's it been so far for you today, Ed? And tell me honestly,' she said warmly as she placed the drinks down and sat opposite me.

Kat knew what a tough time it was for everyone, and that I particularly would struggle with all the change. After her run-in with Finch today, most people would bitch about their situation already, but not Kat.

I told her about my own run-in with Miss Finch and what she said about Noah. Kat listened to everything and then looked thoughtful.

'Anne can't get away with saying Noah isn't allowed in to help when we've got Gracie swanning round. It's pure prejudice.' I hadn't thought of it like that.

It seemed strange hearing Miss Finch being called Anne. Even after being told off for this already this morning, Kat still didn't care about such formalities.

'I need to watch what I say,' she continued.

'But Finch and Tim need to be careful about how they're running the school. A lot of people don't like it.'

'What should I do about her though?'

'Sit tight and watch this space. I think everything will fall into place,' she replied cryptically, and I noticed her smile to herself.

This puzzled me, but Kat quickly changed subject. We chatted for a few minutes and then we stood up for her to see me out. As we were at the doorway of Kat's office, Miss Finch's door flew open. We heard Tim's voice.

'Just remember, Anne, you need to sort this out and sort it NOW or you won't like what happens!'

He slammed her door and stormed away, glaring at us defiantly. As he passed, I noticed his face drop as if he realised that he shouldn't have done that with people watching.

'What the hell was that about?' I asked Kat.

'Like I said,' Kat replied, 'watch this space. Things between those two aren't as rosy as you might think.'

I thought about this as I glanced round the leadership suite. Dylan was sat at his desk in the centre, typing away, seemingly oblivious to what had just happened.

5

Most teachers say you can tell what a school is like to work in by the staff room. Our old staff room was like being at home – comfy sofas, a sink full of dirty dishes but a friendly, warm, comfortable atmosphere. The kettle would be on in moments if someone was having a bad day.

The new staff room, sorry 'gathering suite', was very different. Much like the executive suite, it was very corporate, cold and faceless, without a sofa or a kettle in sight. However, I soon realised they were taking liberties with the word 'suite'. It was a tiny space, which I realised as I entered for the meeting and saw my colleagues crammed in, sitting shoulder to shoulder on fluorescent plastic chairs.

It surprised me to see my colleagues looking so squashed, especially as there were so few people there - mostly leadership team and support staff. For all the money pumped into the new site, the academy was very cautious about staff costs.

I looked around the room. Kat and Dylan sat chatting and eating sweets. Carol Fletcher, the long-term caretaker, stood with a cup of tea in one hand and her mobile phone in the other.

Carol and her husband Brian, the former Maths teacher, had both been at the school for over twenty years. Until Miss Finch arrived and ejected Brian from his job after just two weeks. They still hadn't replaced him; the Science teacher had been doubling up on Science and Maths before summer.

Chalk Gap High has always been a tiny school for our village children from age four through to 18. It is much smaller than the nearest secondary schools in Eastbourne and Seaford and only has around 200 pupils, with one teacher of each subject. There had been a lot of pressure to close it over the years, and Tim clarified that becoming an academy was our only chance of survival.

Tim himself was repeating this for what must have been the twentieth time this year as he started the meeting with Miss Finch at his side. He then introduced 'the woman who had made all of this possible, Miss Finch.' I couldn't believe that this was the same man who'd been tearing a strip off her half an hour ago. The way Tim said it, he was expecting rapturous applause.

Miss Finch didn't look like she cared whether she got applause. She looked around the room, eyeballing each person as she spoke.

'You should feel very privileged to be here today,' she said, addressing the room. 'I have carefully selected those who I believe to be key staff to represent the school for the launch event tomorrow.

'However, when I walk in the room what do I see? I see sweets, sandwiches, drinks, people using mobile phones, people having a chat. You are not on a jolly, ladies and gentlemen. I repeat, you are not on a jolly. You are here to serve your community, but at the moment you are only serving yourselves. Still, I suppose at least you are here on time.'

I glanced at the empty seat next to me. Patrick Herrera - our Head of English, my best friend and my other housemate - was missing. I knew he was still in bed when I left this morning, but I thought he'd make it for the meeting.

Funnily enough, my friendship with him began through him always running late. I did my English Literature degree at Brighton University. It was less than twenty miles away, but my first time travelling out of Chalk Gap regularly.

Awkward and nervous, I sat on my own at the back of each lecture. After a few days, I noticed the guy who always came in 15 minutes late and sat near me on the back row. He would smile and gesture for me to shush as he sneaked in, and we spoke a couple of times to share notes. We were the only two people on our course not to live in student halls – me for obvious reasons, him as he was such a mummy's boy and wanted to stay at home. It wasn't long before we were firm friends.

Patrick stayed on to do teacher training and I got my job here, but he used to visit me and fell in love with Chalk Gap; he said it reminded him of the little village he's from in Spain (yes, he's from Spain – I know he has an Irish name; something to do with his mum and a *Dirty Dancing* obsession). So when the English teacher job came up he went for it and got it, and left his mum's house to move here – though he still visited her multiple times a week ('I can't miss my Spanish food,' is the reason he gives).

He started dating Kat after about a year of working at Chalk Gap High and they moved in together shortly after. It didn't work out, but they said they wanted to stay friends and kept living together. They eventually persuaded me to move in and join them, saying it was to make it less awkward between them, but I knew that was an excuse.

Just as I was thinking about all this, he appeared at the door looking like he was on a night out: skinny black jeans, a white muscle fit top and drowned in aftershave. He had his usual cheeky, sheepish smile, which allowed him to get away with most things. But not this.

'Mr Herrera, thanks for dropping by. We were just talking about lack of staff commitment. What an appropriate time for you to join us.'

So far, so Miss Finch. This was nothing that would bother Patrick.

'I'm sorry I'm late, Miss Finch,' he smiled. He sounded like a naughty pupil, not a teacher. 'I am committed though. I'm committed to looking this good to impress everyone for the launch day tomorrow.' Even for Patrick, this seemed brave.

'Is that a joke, Mr Herrera?' she replied. 'Perhaps you won't be laughing if I tell everyone here about the conversation we had yesterday.'

Patrick's face fell. He looked stunned. What was this? Even Tim looked shocked.

'Anne, I'm not sure if -'

'Lack of professional standards. That's the problem with this school. I noticed it as soon as I arrived here. And you, Mr Herrera, are one of the major culprits. But even I've been surprised by your unprofessional and inappropriate behaviour lately. Maybe we should see what everyone else thinks?'

'Anne, I think we should discuss this with Patrick later instead,' Tim spoke up again.

All eyes were on Patrick. He stood in the doorway but walked forward as if he would say something to her. Then he sat down silently in the seat next to mine, his eyes focused on the floor below him.

'Okay ladies and gentlemen, where was I? Oh yes, the standards we expect for tomorrow...'

I nudged Patrick to check he was okay, but he just carried on staring at the floor. As soon as the meeting finished, he was the first one out of the door without looking at anyone. I gave him a few minutes and then checked on him, but when I got back to the library, I caught sight of him through the window rushing out of the school gates.

6

One of the best things about our village is our beach; it gives you the perfect place to go in a crisis. The other good thing is how close everything is. So it only took me a few minutes to get from school to the beach path underneath East Chalk Cliffs, passing the Hunts' converted farm house and various fields where Gracie rode her horses.

It was mid-afternoon by this point and the rest of the staff were still at school preparing for tomorrow. I was risking Miss Finch's wrath about my 'work in progress' library being up to scratch, but I had to find Patrick and check that he was okay. He'd been there for me plenty of times in the past.

The August sun burned down on the pebble beach as I walked along looking for my best friend. Our beach is usually just occupied by locals and a few well-informed tourists, so compared to Eastbourne and Brighton it was a secret hotspot away from the hordes. Today most people had their own section of beach as I passed the various sunbathers on the shores making the most of the weather. As I got nearer to the village square, I took in the glorious smell of a summer barbecue - the savoury scent reaching me and making my mouth water. I imagined it would be a family or a couple making the most of the sun, so it surprised me to find Patrick sat alone on the beach tending to burgers and sausages on a small disposable grill.

'Hello buddy, just in time!' he shouted to me as I walked across the pebbles to him. 'Here. There's a burger ready for you.'

He prepared two rolls, put tomato ketchup on them and we sat next to each other eating in silence. He knew I was there for him, but he also knew I had no idea what to say. He spoke again first.

'Barbecues are a great way to wind down,' he said, indirectly acknowledging that something had happened earlier. 'They remind me of growing up. We have sand under our feet in Spain though, not these pebbles.'

'Most of our beaches have sand, just not the ones round here I'm afraid.'

'Edward buddy, I miss Spain. I think I should go back there, you know.'

This wasn't like him; he was usually the most laid-back guy I know. There must have been something serious going on. I was just wondering how to voice this when he continued.

'Miss Finch, man... I hate her... I hate her.' His voice lowered in between each pause so I could hardly hear him.

'Patrick, what happened? What was she talking about?'

He sat in silence, looking at the waves coming in. Eventually he answered.

'Something bad, buddy.' Silence again.

I was about to say he could tell me anything when suddenly a seagull swooped down out of nowhere and ripped the burger from Patrick's grasp.

'Oi!' he shouted. He picked up a pebble and threw it, narrowly missing the escaping seagull.

'OI!' he screamed this time, leaping up and launching stone after stone after the bird, before following with a bottle of sun lotion and a flip-flop. 'You want to take everything from me, do you? Well, have it! Have it!'

'Patrick, Patrick – it's gone!' I reached my arm out to stop him. 'It's gone.'

He looked at me stunned; he had even surprised himself. As he hobbled dejectedly across the pebbles to retrieve his flip-flop, I was left wondering what was going on.

7

The seagull incident spoiled the moment on the beach, and I got no more conversation out of Patrick about what was wrong. Instead of coming home with me, he drove to Brighton to see his mum and said he would meet me at the pub later. It was Friday, so that only meant one thing – karaoke night at the Chalk Inn.

My younger brother Alfie runs the pub these days as my mum and dad are technically retired, although mum is always behind the bar and I don't think Dad will ever give up being the pub DJ. His Friday karaoke nights are a long tradition in the village; a weekly event that I would need a doctor's note or a death certificate to miss.

The Chalk Inn, affectionately known as 'The Chalk', is the kind of local pub I'm sure every town and village has. You know the ones – bar in the middle of the room, dim lighting, pool table, jukebox, several old-man regulars littering the place, but where you'll find the beating heart of the community. Okay, so that last one is from Mum's repertoire of phrases, but I thought I'd better include it. But the difference between our pub and the others is being the only pub in our village, we have a captive audience of local drinkers.

Something else that sets The Chalk apart from any run-of-the-mill boozer is my family. We moved down here from our northern hometown of Wigan when I was ten, and the pub's been in our family ever since. My younger brother Alfie took it over from Mum and Dad a couple of years ago; I can never tell if it's his dream job or if he hates every minute. I think he did it to give himself a focus and get mum off his back about ever finding a boyfriend, but, if so, he didn't think it through. All it did was put him in the same building as Mum every day and give her plenty of time to match make for him.

As for my dad, he's the kind of man who talks just a little too loud and is everyone's best mate, whether he has known them fifty years or five minutes. His beer belly pops out of his endless array of floral shirts (all of which are one size too small for him) and he doesn't seem to have noticed that, at five foot five, he is smaller than most people. In his mind, he is the tallest person in any room and the pub is his kingdom.

This makes my mum his queen. You might expect her to be a long-suffering, sensible wife next to Dad, but that's far from accurate. Outwardly, she has the same friendly personality as him and she plays the landlady role to perfection, but she is much less trusting than Dad and thinks she has the measure of everyone that sets foot in the pub. She says, 'I know her game, Edward', or 'she thinks we were born yesterday, that one,' on a pretty much hourly basis.

Unfortunately for me, Mum also has a thing for trying to pair me off at the moment. Any unlucky lady in her early thirties who stumbles into The Chalk can expect a full grilling from my mum (as can any man in his late twenties for my brother). Any visitor not from our village will soon be tricked into disclosing how far away they live, which bus routes they are on, along with a potted CV of their career, family, hobbies and interests. But at least I'm not likely to meet any of these women; it's much more embarrassing when Mum hones in on someone who lives in the village.

On this particular night, I was taking refuge in the pub book corner while cursing Patrick for being late (Kat joins us some Fridays too, but not that night). The book corner was my sole contribution to the running of the pub. Knowing it was there comforted me on my forced Friday night outings, knowing there was a world I could escape to every time I got bored with someone murdering *Summer of 69*.

The books ran round the window ledge in the alcove which housed it in the pub's corner. I perched up on the leather sofa underneath to admire the collection started by me and supplemented by many local donations. My Agatha Christie collection took pride of place – all 66 novels and various short stories - in the 1960s and 70s paperback editions. I'd donated one of my spare collections hoping to get local residents reading the greatest crime writer of all time, but I could tell that most of them hadn't been touched since I last handled them.

These stood among many popular reads half-heartedly donated by people in the village: *The Girl on the Train,* three *Harry Potters,* half a dozen *Mills & Boon* titles, two Dan Browns, *One Day, The Rosie Project, Eleanor Oliphant, Gone Girl,* other female-led thrillers and several books recommended by Richard and Judy which looked like they hadn't been touched. I'm sure Mum had been given them as a Christmas present. I also noticed a beer mat sticking out of one of the books with 'Girl' in the title, being used as a bookmark. Those kind of modern psychological thrillers aren't my cup of tea, but I was glad to see the book corner being used at least.

As I contemplated this, Mum herself appeared carrying a bottle of alcoholic ginger beer for me. She was making a point of bringing over my favourite drink before I'd even asked for it – what did she want? I soon found out.

'You know Edward, I was just serving Emma Oxley, and it got me thinking. She'd be perfect for you!'

As well as running the seafront café, Emma is also Noah's mum. Considering I know her son so well, I've had surprisingly few interactions with Emma. But she always seems very pleasant, is about my age, is pretty for those who notice that kind of thing, and has done a hell of a job bringing up Noah on her own. To say that must have been difficult is an understatement, but Mum wasn't understating anything as she tried to convince me of her worth as a potential girlfriend.

'Honestly, Edward, I don't know how she does it! Looking after that boy and running the cafe, all on her own! And there's no other family around either. She just needs a man in her life to help her.'

Subtlety wasn't one of my mum's strengths. But she raised the bar even higher when I ignored these hints.

'And she's been coming in a lot more lately, I bet she's trying to catch you in here. Speak to her, Edward.'

I didn't point out to Mum that I only ever came in on Friday evenings and it wouldn't take long for anyone to figure this out. Either way, this conversation wasn't one I was in the mood for with the launch day looming, particularly as Emma was sat in earshot across the pub while my dad was up on stage, crooning *Love Is In the Air*.

Emma had never been a regular at Friday karaoke night, but I'd seen her occasionally with a couple of other women, particularly now that Noah was 16 and she could leave him (though he frequently told me she doesn't need to worry; 'what does she think I will do sat at home reading? Paper cut myself to death?'). She was sat on her own tonight though, likely waiting for a late-running friend as I was mine, and seemed occupied by her phone.

'Mum, I'm not going to sit with a lady I hardly know just because we're both on our own. I'm waiting for Patrick and she's waiting for her friends too.'

'You might as well wait together then, hadn't you? Emma won't mind, will you, my darling?'

Suddenly this conversation had moved from a private (ish) to a public one, as mum's voice had leapt across the pub to include Emma in the conversation, who looked up from her phone in mild surprise.

'I was just saying Emma, how my Edward is sat here scaring all our customers away while he waits for his friend, and I guess you're waiting for your friends, so you might as well sit and wait together.'

'Well yes, I suppose he - ,'

'Perfect! Emma, you know he has your boy Noah helping him in the library at the school, don't you? Off you go, Edward. Join her!'

'It's okay, I can come over to Edward -' Emma

started from across the pub, but my mum was having none of it.

'Nonsense, you stay where you are. My son's a gentleman,' Mum said as she ushered me out of my seat. 'They've got a big day tomorrow, but I'm sure he'll tell you all about it, won't you Edward?'

Mum never means to trigger my anxiety, but it surprised me I could still function enough by now to make my way over to Emma's table. From the safety of fiction to the terrors of interaction with a romantic prospect in less than a minute. And just when I thought it couldn't get any worse, Dad's song finished and his speaking voice blasted out across the pub.

'That was *Love is in the Air*, ladies and gentlemen. And love might well be in the air - that's my Ed over there with a new young lady. Go get her, son!'

This would obviously embarrass most people it happened to. You don't know me very well yet, so it's hard for you to imagine the effect something like this would have on me. If you knew me, you wouldn't be surprised to find me locked in the toilet cubicle fifteen minutes later having a panic attack.

8

'Come on, Edward. You need to come out now. Everything's alright.'

My brother Alfie had come to get me. Unable to find the words to speak, my silence was his answer.

'You should have seen what Mum did to me the other week. This good-looking guy was in who she was convinced was gay and single. He was neither. But she'd already taken a drink over to him, told him it was from me, and left my number on his beer mat.'

If this had been anyone else's parents, I'd think they were making the story up to make me feel better. But this was vintage Mum.

I gave in. 'Okay, yours is worse.'

'That's not the end. His girlfriend came in a few minutes after and was glaring at me all night. I got a text from her after they left telling me to leave her boyfriend alone.'

We laughed together on either side of the cubicle door, in shared embarrassment and love for our mum and dad. He never said, but I knew

Alfie understood. He didn't have quite the same difficulties as me but he'd had to suffer through coming out, and had the same well meaning, utterly frustrating but ultimately loving parents I did.

'Don't freak out, but mum might be on to something with this Emma you know.'

'Are you joking? I ran away from her and locked myself in the loo. I can't ever look at her again.'

'Well, you will have to look at her 'cos she's got you a drink. It's sat at her table waiting for you.'

'What, are you serious?'

'Yep. She came and found me at the pool table. She told me what happened and suggested I sent Mum on a break. She even insisted on buying you a drink.'

I thought about what he said for a minute, but Alfie still wasn't done.

'I know it's difficult for you, Edward. But get yourself out there. She seems nice and you already know Noah, so just talk to her. So I'll see you out there, alright?'

At that moment, the very idea of even stepping out of the cubicle seemed impossible, let alone sitting with the attractive woman who witnessed my retreat into here. But Alfie never gave up easily.

'Oh, and your hide and seek act is old news. Brian Fletcher's out there making an idiot of himself again. Cursing your Head Teacher and saying he'll ruin the open day tomorrow. I might have to throw him out soon.'

I was grateful to have something to think about other than my embarrassment and anxiety. By all accounts, Brian Fletcher's drunken outbursts had got much worse in the last few weeks. And as my family runs the only pub in our village, those accounts seemed accurate.

'Okay Alfie, cheers. I'll be out in a minute.'

If you want to keep track of people who had an issue with Miss Finch, Brian Fletcher should be top of your list. I mentioned earlier that he was the Maths teacher at school until recently. There's a Brian teaching at every school - or maybe every school Miss Finch isn't in charge of. You know the one – been there about a hundred years, repeating the same old Maths or Science lessons and moaning about everything in the school.

Miss Finch was gunning for him as soon as she arrived. Poor old Brian didn't know what hit him. I've never found out exactly what happened. But within three days of Miss Finch arriving, Brian was grumbling to anyone who would listen about victimisation. Then he suddenly went quiet for a couple of days, saying if anyone asked him that he wasn't allowed to talk about it. By the second week, we barely saw him; he retreated from the staff room (his former stomping ground), although he was summoned to Miss Finch's office several times and shouted at (Dylan is a great spy).

Then on the Friday of that week we received an email from Dylan on Miss Finch's behalf to tell us it was Brian's last day. He'd mutually agreed with the academy to take early retirement. Nobody could believe it. Many people thought Brian had outstayed his welcome, but Miss Finch managed in two weeks what no one else had in twenty years. She had got rid of him in less time than it took Carol to get rid of the wasps' nests infesting the school garden. How she'd managed it was a mystery.

But it wasn't a mystery for long. Brian's visits to the pub had become more frequent and more rowdy, telling anyone who would listen about how he'd been bullied out of his job. And tonight was no exception. I came out of the toilets to see the end of his 'performance' of Simple Minds' 'Don't You Forget About Me' – grossly out of tune as he slurred his words, staggering and stumbling round the stage. As the song drew to a close, he carried on using the microphone to address the pub.

'And I'll tell you who better not forget about me – that Finch woman! She'll get what's coming to her-'

'Alright Brian, that's enough!' Not missing a beat, Alfie was straight up on stage. 'Come on, mate, time to go home!'

Brian tried to dodge my brother as he made a drink gesture out into the pub. 'And cheers for the drinks, love!' Was that to my mum? She would not be accepting that thank you very gratefully, I knew that.

Brian struggled and shouted as my brother tried to get him off the stage, but Alfie wasn't alone for long.

'BRIAN! What the hell are you playing at?'

Carol Fletcher was in the doorway and her voice commanded her husband (and, in fact, the whole pub) to stop. Brian's firing had been embarrassing for her, still working as the school caretaker. Carol is what my mum calls a 'salt of the earth' woman, which seems to translate as dependable, reliable, says exactly what she thinks and you wouldn't want to get on the wrong side of her.

That's why everyone was surprised when she never said a word in public about Miss Finch and Brian's dismissal. She still came in to work with the same pleasant smile that she always had. She certainly wasn't smiling as she slammed her handbag on the table and stormed over to drag Brian off the stage.

'Brian Fletcher, I swear you'll be the death of me. Get your backside out of this pub now!' The toilets are at the side of the pub near the door, so they had to pass me as they left. Carol looked angry, upset and embarrassed.

As she pushed Brian through the door, then turned back to look at me and whispered, 'Edward, that Finch woman has got a lot to answer for.' I looked back in sympathy but didn't quite know how to respond.

'And I'll tell you something, my Brian's right about one thing.' She lowered her voice even more and looked straight at me.

'She will get what's coming to her.'

9

With the drama over, everyone in the pub went back to their normal business. I looked over at Emma's table and noticed it empty, with her bag gone. I didn't know what Alfie was talking about before, but he must have been mistaken; of course she didn't want to have a drink with me – she'd gone.

Or so I thought. 'Edward, over here!' I turned to see Emma sat in the book corner, with a glass of wine in front of her and the book I'd spotted earlier in her hand. 'Come sit down, I got you a drink!' she said as she gestured to the bottle of alcoholic ginger beer in front of her. I glanced over at the bar to Alfie, who winked at me.

'I hope you don't mind me moving us over here, I just love this book corner.' She glanced over her shoulder at the books and smiled, as she patted the seat next to her on the leather sofa for me to sit, 'I normally sit here but you beat me to it tonight, then your mum got you to join me before I could say anything.'

'Yeah, sorry about her,' I said as I sank into the soft leather next to her, noticing for the first time how comfortable the sofa was.

'Nothing to apologise for, a mum's got to look out for her son no matter how old they get,' she replied as she moved her glass toward mine. 'Anyway, cheers Edward – it's lovely to chat with you properly.'

She was ignoring my embarrassing hideout in the toilets, which was more than fine by me. I felt comfortable enough to ask her the question I'd been dying to ask since I came back.

'So, you're the person using my book corner? I spotted the beer mat bookmark earlier.'

She looked down at the book in front of her and chuckled. 'You got me. Noah loves all those old mysteries like you do, but give me a modern thriller with a woman in danger and an unreliable narrator any day.'

This seemed to be the direction of many modern crime thrillers but I had to make a case for my idol. 'Agatha Christie *invented* the unreliable narrator – modern crime fiction wouldn't even exist without her.'

'You sound just like Noah,' she replied. 'I suppose, I just find them a bit old and dusty.'

What? 'They are classics. So much suspense, amazing plot twists and incredibly smart detectives. Honestly, Emma, there's so many classics you need to read – *And Then There Were None, Murder on the Orient Express, The Murder of Roger Ackroyd* to name only a few. Probably the three greatest crime novels of all time.'

'*And Then There Were None*? On the island where they all get killed one by one? I saw the adaptation of that on BBC a few years ago, it was great.'

'Yes it was, but honestly – read the book. You won't be disappointed.'

'Okay, I'll give it a go after I've finished this.' She waved her book in front of her to reference it. 'I'm sure Noah has that one.'

I laughed to myself at the thought of Noah not owning a copy of the classic mystery. 'I'm sure he has.'

After that, we spent a little while debating over our favourite novels, making promises to the other one to read specific books. I had to give Mum her due on this one. Sitting with Emma wasn't a bad idea after all. After breaking the ice talking about crime fiction, our conversation turned more general.

'Can you believe Carol's husband earlier? He's the one who got fired from school, isn't he?' Emma asked, enjoying the gossip. 'Carol's lovely when she comes in the café, but he wasn't very nice about Noah last parents evening.' Her rapid fire conversation reminded me of her son's.

I sat down and filled her in on what I knew. She didn't seem to have heard about Brian from Noah, but to me he'd named Brian as the number one suspect in Miss Finch's supposedly inevitable murder. She never mentioned this, so I didn't either; I didn't know her well enough to talk about her son like that. Or so I thought.

'I just wanted to say thank you, Edward, for all you do for Noah. I know he's not always easy, but he loves helping you in the library. I don't know what he'd be like if he didn't have that.'

I answered graciously before my brain caught up and realised I rarely know how to take compliments.

'It's alright. To be honest, I like the company. And he knows that library inside out, even better than I do.'

Emma wrapped her hands round her drink and smiled. 'His brain is like Wikipedia. I don't know where he gets it from, it isn't me!'

She paused and laughed; she looked so animated when she talked about her son. 'Seriously though, Edward, I'm glad I've got to speak to you - I've wanted to say thank you for ages. He thinks the world of you, you're all he ever talks about.'

'With Noah, I doubt that very much.'

'Oh Edward, you know him so well!' She laughed

so much this time she nearly spat her wine out. 'I love him to pieces but all I ever hear is murder this, detective that. I sometimes feel like I'm on the Orient Express I hear so much about Agatha Christie!'

'If he has his way, in a few years' time, you'll have the modern version of her on your hands.'

As well as thinking life was a murder mystery plot, Noah had been working on his very own mystery novel. It was amazing how close Noah's path seemed to be to my own when I was younger – though hopefully Noah will succeed on his. Patrick told me it was a project for them to practice their creative writing, but to Noah it was his masterpiece. He was taking it so seriously; he hadn't even discussed what it was about, which was unusual for him.

'Oh, his story?' she blurted. 'Yes, either that or he'll become a serial killer.'

I was taken aback for a second. She had meant it as a joke, but she didn't know that this remark closely mirrored Gracie's insult that morning. It was unusual for the average sixteen–year-old to develop such an obsession with old-fashioned murder mysteries, and you can see why it made Noah a target for bullies – as it had for me at the same age.

Emma might not have known about this, but she could tell I had zoned out for a second.

'Are you worried you're his next victim? Encyclopaedia to the head? Paper cut to death?'

'It's funny, Noah uses that exact phrase all the time.' I relaxed and laughed with her. 'Maybe you're the one I need to watch out for. Maybe he gets it from you.'

Was I flirting with her? I'm not usually very good with people I don't know well (as you've already seen), but there was something about Emma which made me feel at ease. Maybe it was the connection I had to Noah, maybe it was her down-to-earth humour, or maybe because I found her strangely attractive.

I didn't think about the point further as my phone buzzed with a message from Patrick.

'Sorry buddy I'm not going to make it tonight. Cheers for finding me at the beach. Will explain everything soon.'

I sent a reply saying I guessed I'd see him at home. But this was getting strange. A night out was usually the answer to all of Patrick's troubles, and he never missed our Fridays in the Chalk. More often than not, he ended up in a taxi to Eastbourne or Brighton to carry on partying. At 32, Patrick probably needed to grow up a little and settle down; he wasn't always the most responsible person for a teacher. Had Miss Finch found out something, or was she threatening him? She had easily got rid of Brian, so it wasn't inconceivable that Patrick could be next.

'A penny for them.'

I was so lost in this digression that I'd forgotten Emma was there for a moment.

'Sorry, what did you say?'

'Your thoughts, a penny for them!'

And then I did something I didn't expect. I told Emma, who I was having my first proper conversation with, everything that had happened that day and how worried I was about Patrick.

After I finished the story, she tried to reassure me.

'I don't think she'll get rid of him just because she got rid of Carol's husband. They're two different cases. Fletcher is an old grump who'd lost interest in his job, anyone can see that. Your friend Patrick is great for that school – he's young, smart, good looking…'

She stopped herself and looked embarrassed. It didn't seem like she meant to say that in front of me. There was an awkward silence, which she eventually filled.

'You're an incredible friend,' she said out of nowhere.

'What, to Patrick?'

'Yes, I meant to Patrick mainly. But to Noah too.'

'Well, I'm not allowed to be friends with Noah, as such.'

'You know what I mean. Since Dad died, I've always said Noah and I don't need anyone else – it's just us two against the world. But I'm glad he's got you. And either way, you're allowed to be my friend, aren't you?'

'I suppose I am, yes.'

'That settles it then!' she replied, smiling. 'Well, my new friend, I've enjoyed our chat tonight. Come and find me in the café soon, I never see you there.'

With that, she said her goodbyes and left. Emma had barely left the pub when mum came racing over to the table.

'See, what did I tell you?'

'Okay mum, Emma and I are friends. But let's leave it at that.'

But funnily enough, my mind didn't want to leave it at that. I'd really enjoyed speaking to Emma, and it wasn't like anything I'd felt before. But it competed for attention with all the other things going round my mind.

Most of them involved Miss Finch – mainly her comments about the library, but not just that. There were Kat's views on her bullying ways, and the various threats to her from Tim Hunt, and Brian and Carol Fletcher. Tim's in a professional capacity, the Fletchers' not.

If Miss Finch wasn't already the most disliked woman in the village, she seemed to be now. At that point, I didn't know Noah's prediction would come true, but even then there were several suspects lined up.

10

I looked at the time on my phone. 7:33AM. I had been awake for about three hours, lying there unable to sleep with my thoughts weighing down on me.

'I trust this is a work in progress.'

'I trust this is a work in progress.'

'I trust this is a work in progress.'

There were so many things on my mind when I went to bed last night, but for the last three hours this was the one that I couldn't get out of my head.

'I trust this is a work in progress.'

Miss Finch's words to me about the brand new library. It wasn't a work in progress. I'd spent weeks making sure I got it just right – not a book out of place, not a display that wasn't eye catching. Until she spoke those words, I was actually pleased with it. And that's an enormous achievement for someone who never stops analysing everything.

But now I had cause to be concerned. Today

the library would be under scrutiny as part of the launch event, and Miss Finch had made it clear she considered the library one of the key attractions.

We had to be at school for ten in the morning, to give us two hours more preparation before the launch day started. Those two hours would surely be taken up by more pointless meetings, more drop-ins from Miss Finch, and no chance to fix whatever she thought was wrong. I had to go in before that.

After getting dressed I was rushing round the house trying to find my shoes. One issue with sharing with other people is your things are always getting moved. As I bounded into the living room, I found Kat on the sofa in her fluffy pink dressing gown, watching *Unsolved Mysteries* on Netflix.

'You'd love this show, Ed. I bet you'd solve every case.'

I ignored her as I scanned round the room for my shoes. 'Why are you up so early?'

'I could say the same,' she retorted. 'Was it you banging round about 5am? It woke me up and I've been awake since.'

I'd heard it myself and was even tempted to see if it was him, but my anxiety attack had other ideas. 'No, it wasn't me. Was it Patrick? He was a no-show at the pub last night.'

'Must be, but there was loads of going up and down the stairs and I heard the outside door. He probably had a girl back,' she said as she rolled her eyes. A small part of her would always be his ex-girlfriend, not just his housemate and friend.

'Maybe,' I replied distractedly as I gave up my search. 'Kat, where on earth are my shoes?'

'If you didn't have so many books piled up everywhere you'd be able to find them,' she remarked half-heartedly as she focused on the TV screen.

I stopped for a second and took in the surrounding scene. Our bookcase was in the room's corner, the oak shelves barely visible underneath literally hundreds of books piled up on top of each other. Agatha Christie (five complete collections, as I'd told Emma), Dorothy L Sayers, Ngaio Marsh, M.C. Beaton, Simon Brett and others all filled the shelf space in the same way they filled my heart – probably over-spilling a bit too much. Then around the room in various piles, the cause of Kat's complaint, were more recent contributions to the genre – Victoria Dowd, Benedict Brown, Mairi Chong, Debbie Young – some waiting to be read, some already a treasured part of my self-compiled history of classic mysteries. I felt a pang of sadness as I considered these authors scattered around our living room - all independently published or with a small publisher - and I wondered what could have been.

Kat broke me from my spell. 'Anyway, why are you going in so early? I thought I was the workaholic.'

'Just got things to finish,' I called out as I ran back upstairs to find a spare pair instead. Sharing a house, even with your friends, is frustrating sometimes, but it beats living with my family above the pub, and school librarian wages wouldn't get me much of a place of my own.

I walked as briskly as I could the ten minutes to get to school. Carol would surely be there this early: as the school caretaker with no other cleaning staff afforded to her, she would have a lot to do. And she was always there - as if she lived there. Though I think I might too if I had Brian at home.

Like most staff, Carol lived in the village and walked to work unless the weather was bad. I expected to find the school car park empty as I arrived just after eight, but, to my dismay, there was already one car there when I arrived. Miss Finch's. I couldn't believe my terrible luck; how was I meant to sort out the library if she would be looking over my shoulder?

Just when I thought things couldn't get any worse, I heard a voice behind me.

'Morning, Mr Crisp!' I turned around to see the

owner of the voice jump down off the wall, as he waved like air traffic control bringing a plane in.

'Noah, what are you doing here?'

'I waited up for my mum last night. She said she chatted to you and you were nice to her. So I decided you shouldn't have to do without me just because of Miss Finch. I've come to help you before she gets here.'

I sighed. 'Erm Noah, that's her car over there.'

'Is it?' He looked puzzled. 'I don't know who drives which car. But it's been there the whole time since I got here an hour ago.'

An hour? He'd been there since 7am, waiting for me?

'Miss Fletcher hasn't though,' he continued. 'She only got here about ten minutes ago, she ran past me like she was late.'

That wasn't like Carol at all, I thought she'd have been here ages ago. Right on cue, Carol herself came running out of the school building towards us.

'Oh Edward, Edward, help, do something! It's Miss Finch!'

She was in a terrible state, but it was barely 8am. Surely Miss Finch hadn't now sacked Carol before even having breakfast. This didn't seem like that though - Carol was panicked.

'Carol, what's the matter?' I replied. 'What's Miss Finch done now?'

'No, no, it's not that,' Carol spluttered. 'Edward, the thing is, she's dead.'

11

'Sorry Carol, what did you just say?' I couldn't believe my ears.

'You heard me. She's DEAD!' she screamed.

This was one of those moments in life where the news you get is so shocking you just don't know what to say. Luckily (or unluckily, as you will now see), Noah replied for me.

'This is perfect!'

Carol looked at him in disbelief. It may say more about me that I completely understood what he meant, but, either way, I thought I'd better step in and explain.

'He doesn't mean perfect as in it's good.'

I hadn't helped Carol to understand. 'What else does "perfect" mean?'

'He just means that… that…' I've got to be honest, I was struggling. Luckily (or again, maybe unluckily), Noah came to the rescue.

'Don't worry, Mrs Fletcher, you don't know what I meant. It's just that Mr Crisp and I like murder mysteries, and I predicted Miss Finch would be a murder victim on the new school launch day. Which is today, and you've just told us it's happened. So I was quite pleased.'

I watched Carol's already shocked and shaken expression turn to one of complete horror as she looked at us both.

I attempted to explain. 'Well, he doesn't mean he's pleased as such…' I had nothing.

Carol continued just to stare at us.

'You…' She honed in on Noah. 'You were stood outside waiting when I got here. And you're always listening in the café when I'm talking to your mum. You… did *you* do this?'

Noah smiled and replied calmly. 'Oh no, of course I didn't. I can see why you'd think that, but it's never the detectives.'

She looked more confused than ever.

'He thinks he and I will be amateur detectives and "solve the case", so to speak,' I interjected quickly. Noah had walked to the main doors and was peering into the foyer. I seized the moment to remind Carol about why he acted like that.

'This is obviously an enormous shock for everyone, Carol,' I started. 'But remember Noah is sixteen and has his own particular needs.'

'Brian always told me when he taught him

there's something not right about him,' she replied. 'So when he started saying those strange things, and I remembered he was outside the entire time -'

'Carol, Noah's different to us. This is his way of showing his shock.'

She looked at me, visibly processing everything. 'You're right, love. He's alright, and his mum's lovely. I just, just... can't... Edward. How on earth did this happen?'

'I'm not sure yet. Are you sure she's definitely dead? We need to ring 999.'

'She's definitely dead love, I won't forget that in a hurry!' she replied through pacing backwards and forwards. 'That's what I came out here to do.'

'Okay, so let's ring the police then that's our bit done.' I wasn't used to being the one taking charge of situations like this (not that situations like this normally happened) but I just found myself doing it. However, I hadn't counted on Noah's return to the conversation.

'No, don't ring the police yet,' he said as he walked back over to us.

'What?'

'Don't ring them,' he repeated. 'The village police won't know what to do.'

I couldn't believe this. 'Noah, we don't even

have village police. But we dial 999 and Sussex Police will come from Lewes or wherever they are based.'

'Yes, of course,' he replied. 'But we just need to have a look at the crime scene first for our own investigation.'

'This isn't a murder mystery, this is real life! We are not professionals and we can't investigate a crime scene. Now Carol, please ring 999.'

Carol fumbled with her phone and then stopped and looked at me.

'He's right,' she said.

'Thank you!' I replied. 'Noah, that's two adults telling you we need to ring for the police immediately. I know you mean well, but this is serious.'

'No, I mean he's right,' she said, pointing at Noah. 'We'll ring the police in five minutes but I think you two should see the body first.'

12

I couldn't believe that instead of ringing the police, Carol was ushering us into the leadership suite to see Miss Finch's dead body.

'We shouldn't be doing this,' I protested.

'Look, love. Do you know what the police round here spend their time doing?' she asked. 'Wasting the taxpayer's money, hassling good, hard-working people with rubbish about being drunk and disorderly.' Brian must have had an unpleasant experience (or several) with Sussex Police.

But she wasn't through. 'Edward, how long have I known you? I remember you as a baby! And yes, you're a little odd, but you're the smartest guy I know. And this young man,' she gestured at Noah, 'is even odder, so that probably means he's even smarter. So if you two know all about these murder mysteries, there's no harm in you having a look for five minutes and seeing what's what. Now get in there and see what you can find, I don't want them blaming me 'cos I found her.'

I tried to process what she'd just said. In fact, I tried to process everything that had happened in the last five minutes. Miss Finch had been found dead, exactly when and where Noah said she would. And now we were having an illicit sneak peek at the crime scene before we called the police.

'I know we've had a shock, but I think we've lost our minds here,' I tried to reason. 'I'm not taking a 16-year-old to see a dead body.'

'Oh don't worry, Sir, I'll explain to my Mum that I wanted to, she knows what I'm like,' Noah replied as he looked at the door in front of us in excitement.

'Yes she does, to be fair,' Carol said, backing him up. 'I know Emma, if there's any problem, you haven't taken him – I have. Just a quick check and then we'll call the police.'

I wasn't going to win this one. We moved into the leadership suite and I looked straight over to Miss Finch's glass office. She was at the meeting table in the centre of the room, slumped forward over the table.

'Okay, Miss and Sir, you need to listen carefully,' Noah instructed. What now?

'We need to do this properly. Make sure we touch nothing. We don't want to contaminate the crime scene, we could obscure the murderer's prints.'

'And we don't want them blaming us!' Carol said.

I saw that she really didn't trust the police.

'We don't even know it's a murder yet,' I pointed out. 'It could be a heart attack.'

'Just wait for it, love - when you see her, you won't think it's a heart attack then.'

'Miss, you open the door,' Noah instructed. 'You've already done that naturally as part of your job so your fingerprints are already on there. But nobody else touch anything.'

Carol took a deep breath as she opened the door. Despite choosing to bring us here, she really looked like she didn't want to go into this room a second time.

'I thought she was asleep at first,' she said. 'She was here so early that it's possible. But then I realised if there was anyone that wasn't the napping-at-work type, it was Miss Finch. So I checked on her.'

I walked in behind Carol and got a full look at the scene for the first time. You always think of murder scenes as a bloody mess, described in gruesome detail in modern police procedural novels, and conveniently left out of many of the more traditional or cozy murder mysteries.

This one was nothing like any of those. Like Miss Finch's office itself, it was plain, clean and lifeless. As Carol had suggested, we might not even have known Miss Finch was dead at first. But she was.

She lay flat, slumped across her meeting table, face to the side and arms spread out. There were various papers and files on the table which she had landed on and spread across in disarray. On the floor beside her lay a crushed plastic cup. Otherwise, there seemed to be no other evidence of foul play. Her office desk sat immaculate and empty behind her. She had obviously gone straight to work at the meeting table when she arrived.

'How did you know she was dead?' Noah asked Carol as he took photos of the scene. I wasn't entirely comfortable with this, but I thought it best to ignore. 'You didn't touch the body, did you?'

'Of course I didn't,' Carol replied. 'Like I said, wait 'til you see her face.'

'Not you, Noah,' I said firmly, putting my arm out to block him. That was one image I would spare him. 'I'll do it.'

He looked disappointed but didn't argue. I reluctantly stepped forward to see the contorted, wretched features I still see in my mind now when I can't sleep at night.

Carol stopped and paused, looking straight at me. I had just remembered her threat in the pub last night and, from Carol's face, I could tell she had too. She looked away, guilty and embarrassed.

'We need to establish what facts we can,' Noah

said.

I sighed. If we were going to do this, I thought I should be the one leading the investigation at least.

'Okay Noah, you're right. I want you to use that phone of yours to note what I say.'

He nodded enthusiastically – this was right up his street.

'No sign of forced entry into the room or any other sign that someone was here. She appears to have gone straight to the meeting table on arrival. Papers on table and under her head suggest that she was reading them when she died.'

'So what happened?' Carol asked.

'Crushed plastic cup suggests she was holding it while she died,' I continued in reply. 'Cup is empty with tiny traces of liquid, and no sign of any spillage. This suggests that she drank from the cup and had finished it, but the crushing suggests the effects were immediate.'

'She was poisoned!' Noah jumped in. 'She must have been. The poison was in either the water or the cup itself, and, as soon as she drank it, she died.'

'We can't assume anything, but it's a possibility,' I confirmed. I'm not sure who I was keeping this calm act up for - Noah, Carol or myself.

Despite my reply, I was sure at that moment that it was poisoning and someone we knew was responsible. Poisoned water or cup was the likely murder weapon.

'Carol, do you know who had access to the new security passes?'

'Yes, Miss Finch asked me to work with Dylan to get them set up. The list is in my room, but we have to head there anyway to check the CCTV footage.'

I felt that we were getting in deeper and deeper. 'Okay, let's go to your office. But we need to phone the police – we've left it long enough already.'

As we were leaving, I felt the urge to turn back and take one last look at the full scene. When I did, I spotted something under the table near the body.

'Hang on,' I said as I went to get a proper look. 'We might have another piece of evidence, Noah. It looks like a shirt button.'

13

'I'm so glad we have a clue to the murderer's identity!' Noah was delighted with this latest development and couldn't stop talking about it as we waited outside Carol's office door while she rang the police.

'I'm sure it belongs to Mr Hunt or Dylan,' I replied. 'They both go in there all the time. In fact, I saw Mr Hunt there yesterday.'

I cast my mind back to seeing Tim storm his way out of Miss Finch's office. Like Carol's threat in the pub, it now appeared in a different light.

'Right, they're on the way,' Carol said as her door burst open. 'They'll be coming from Lewes station so we have a bit of time to check the CCTV and the ID list.'

'Our list of suspects!' Noah squealed in delight. I feared that he was enjoying this too much and hadn't grasped the real life ramifications of it. I knew the police would want to speak to us, and then I'd have to get him back home to Emma as soon as I could.

'Here we go,' Carol got ready to read from the list. 'So far, only the people who needed to be here yesterday have the new swipe cards.'

'Great, that narrows it down,' I responded. 'And does everyone in this list have access to everywhere, including Miss Finch's office?'

'Yes they do,' Carol confirmed. 'The new system just seems like a way to show off how much money they're spending rather than make the school more secure. They're ridiculous, they haven't even got the alarms working yet. Anyway, none of the offices in that leadership suite, including Miss Finch's, have locks on the doors. You only need access to the suite itself, which everyone in work yesterday had, and you can walk into any office you like.'

'Okay, so who had access then?' I asked. 'Noah, note this down for me.'

'Right, so the names on here...,' she started. 'Obviously Miss Finch herself... Dylan Spence... Kat Parker... me, you... Patrick Herrera... Tim Hunt.'

'Our list of suspects!' Noah squealed again as he hurriedly typed the names into his phone.

'Wait, that can't be right,' Carol said. 'Someone else was issued a full working security pass without me knowing. Looks like Tim had one made for Gracie.'

'Of course she's a suspect!' Noah exclaimed as he typed again. 'There's always a really obviously nasty suspect. She won't be the killer though.'

'This isn't a game, love,' Carol said. 'But yes, she could go anywhere she wanted. Right, let's look at that CCTV.'

I was shocked for a moment about Gracie, but on reflection not surprised. Tim was constantly undermining all the school's rules and policies - flouting them for his own ends or bending them for Gracie. Carol interrupted my thoughts.

'We won't get much from the CCTV.'

'Oh, why's that?'

'The lot of it's gone. Everything from last night onwards has already been deleted, and it's not been recording since.'

14

I needed to think. I had so many questions in my head about Miss Finch's death.

Who deleted the CCTV, was it the murderer?

Was Miss Finch poisoned, and if so how?

How long had she been dead and when was the poison placed in her office?

Who did the button belong to and was it related to her murder?

Was it definitely one of the people with access to the room, or could someone else have got hold of their ID? (Brian with Carol's, for example)

We were waiting in the staff room to be interviewed, and my head was spinning. It was two hours since Carol had phoned the police and we had been joined by the other suspects – though I think they were still referring to us as witnesses at this point.

Ordinary uniformed police had arrived first,

and they let the other staff arrive naturally at 10am, so we had everyone present who had been in the school yesterday. The only difference was that they rang Tim in advance and asked him to come to school with Gracie. This is what he was moaning about when I drifted back into the room after running through my list of questions in my head.

'Honestly, it's ridiculous, bringing an innocent teenage girl into this. I've known the DCI for over twenty years, I'll be calling him about this.'

'Tim, we are all innocent,' Kat Parker said. 'The fact is Gracie was here yesterday, so they just need to speak to each of us to see what we know.'

Gracie herself was sat next to her dad, completely engrossed in her phone and uninterested in everything else. She probably wasn't even listening. I knew that Gracie wasn't a very nice young lady, but I wasn't sure if she was capable of murder. It was an enormous shock when Agatha Christie had a young girl as the murderer in one of her novels, but that was almost a century ago. It's a sad reflection of our times that it would be less of a shock these days.

Zoning out again, this reconsideration of Gracie made me look around the room at the other suspects and consider each one of them as a possible murderer.

Her father, Tim Hunt, Head of Governors, still

sat name-dropping the Chief of Police. Arrogant, used to getting his own way, possibly as much of a bully as his daughter. And we saw him leaving Miss Finch's office rather angry yesterday. But a killer?

Kat Parker, our Deputy Head. Always the voice of reason, and probably the calmest of everyone in the room right now. She had wanted Miss Finch's job, didn't get it, and had been made to feel inferior since. Her career at our school would soon be over if Miss Finch had anything to do with it. But Kat was a nice, normal, reasonable woman, as well as my housemate and good friend. There was no way she could have done it. Was there?

Dylan Spence. Miss Finch's P.A. was definitely the person in the room I knew the least about. He was brilliantly efficient, had settled in really well and was well-liked by everyone. And a white lie to an old lady didn't make him a murderer. But I didn't have much to go off either way.

Carol seemed heavily involved already. She'd found the body, knew the most about the security systems, and had openly said to me the night before that Miss Finch would get what was coming to her. The poison could be one of her cleaning products. And her husband had even more of a grudge against Finch. Could she have done it for him, or were they in on it together? Had he got hold of her school keys and ID last night in a drunken rage without her knowing?

And finally, Noah. Noah was busily writing away in his notepad and seemed to be having a whale of a time. He had an unhealthy obsession with murder mysteries, but this was his Asperger's. I suspected Noah the least, as I knew in my heart that he couldn't have done this. But would the police?

Looking around the room, it seemed insane that one of my colleagues or students could have committed this crime. I love Agatha Christie, as you know, but normal people in normal tiny villages don't go around murdering Head Teachers, no matter how mean they are.

No, someone I know must have murdered Miss Finch. But something didn't feel right.

I looked around the room again and at the empty seat next to Kat. And then I realised. How had I not seen this before? Patrick wasn't there.

He'd been in an awful state and not turned up to the pub last night; Miss Finch seemed to know something incriminating about him. And now she had been murdered and he was missing.

15

The police constable guarding the staff room had allowed Kat and Dylan to make us all a cup of tea, which they were now handing out to everyone. Carol was being interviewed, and I was still waiting. They had kept the two of us until last. They had seen all the adults already, but asked everyone to wait in case they needed them again.

'Erm, I'm good thanks,' Gracie sniped as Dylan tried to pass a tea to her. 'I don't want to go the same way as Finch.'

'I hardly think we would take everyone out in one mass poisoning,' replied Dylan, who looked somewhere between hurt and offended.

'Just being cautious, Grace, my darling, aren't you?' Of course, her father would come straight to her defence. 'She's always been very sensible, Dylan, no offence intended I'm sure.'

Gracie rolled her eyes to show that she didn't care if offence had been taken. Dylan then attempted to pass one tea to Tim himself.

'I'll give it a miss too, if you don't mind.'

'Oh, come on, Tim!' Kat started. 'We made it ourselves, what do you think we've done to it?'

As Tim reminded Kat about the appropriate way to speak to him in front of his daughter and their colleagues, my mind wandered to Patrick again.

I refused to believe that he had anything to do with Miss Finch's murder, but why wasn't he here? Had he done a runner? If it had nothing to do with the murder, why had he disappeared? Then I remembered something he said the day before. About wanting to move back to Spain. Surely he wouldn't take such drastic action over being humiliated in the staff room. What was he hiding?

'Don't worry Sir, it's never the suspect that goes mysteriously missing after the murder.'

Noah's comment brought me back into the room. 'Sorry Noah, what?'

'Mr Herrera. You've been staring at the empty chair for ten minutes, so I guessed that's what you're thinking about. Plus, as a fellow detective, that's what I was wondering too. We must consider the obvious suspects first.'

Across the room, Gracie smirked, looking ready to speak. I could feel myself starting to get angry with how blatant she was being, even in front of the staff. Memories of my own cruel bullying came flooding back to me. But surely she wouldn't insult Noah in front of everyone in the room? No, she was cleverer than that.

'Daddy, did Mr Herrera kill Miss Finch?'

'Tim, I don't think she should -' Kat started.

'Of course not, darling,' he replied. 'Well, actually, I don't know. I hope not.'

'Tim!' Kat was unsurprisingly the one who spoke up. 'We can't be accusing each other like that, we don't know anything. We don't know why Patrick isn't here. We don't even know how Miss Finch died yet, and they've asked us not to discuss our interviews with each other.'

This gave Grace a cue for more mischief. 'Daddy, do you think the poison came from Miss Fletcher's cupboard?'

It was lucky that Carol was out being interviewed. She'd be poisoning Gracie next if she heard that.

'Tim, considering your connections with the DCI, I'm sure the police would allow you and Gracie to wait in another room so you can have some privacy?' Kat said firmly. 'It's probably too upsetting for Gracie to be here amongst all of this talk about what happened.'

'If he's staying, I'm staying, Daddy,' Gracie said, gesturing over to Noah. As the squabbling between Kat and Tim continued with Gracie looking delighted in between, Noah took the opportunity to speak to me with no one listening.

'Maybe we should still consider Gracie after all, Sir. Agatha Christie did the young girl killer once, so it could be the same in this murder mystery too.'

Having had this thought too, I felt annoyance at myself for relying on the same fictional tropes as Noah. In hindsight, I think this coloured what I said to Noah next.

'Noah,' I tried to speak firmly. 'This is not a murder mystery, it is a real life tragedy. There is a real life person, your Head Teacher, lying dead down the corridor. This is a very serious crime which needs to be investigated by the police. Not by us, Noah. I'm a school librarian and you're a sixteen-year-old boy. We need to leave it to the people who know what they are doing. Okay?'

He looked me straight in the eye, like I had completely betrayed him.

'Okay Sir, that's fine.'

I felt guilty. Had I gone too far? I didn't want to upset him, but we'd already got in too deep and we had to stop now. I had to make him understand that this wasn't a game – we didn't get to play Poirot and Hastings. As he looked ahead into thin air, I could see Gracie smirking to herself. Great. She had obviously heard, and I had just embarrassed him in front of his bully.

I didn't get much chance to think about this further as Carol appeared at the doorway.

'They're asking for you next, Edward.'

'How did it go?' I asked, not sure what answer to expect in front of everyone else.

'The interviews are in the dining hall, I'll walk back down with you,' she replied hastily and motioned for me to follow her.

'That's okay isn't it, Officer?' she asked the young, bored Constable on the door without waiting for an answer from him as she walked straight past.

'I've known PC Wood for years, I know his mother,' she explained. 'I can tell you lots of tales about him growing up. He won't say no to me easily.'

'How did it go then, Carol?' I whispered, making sure PC Wood was definitely out of earshot – even though Carol hadn't bothered to do the same.

'Fine. Bit of a kid this detective is, he can't be any older than you.'

I didn't point out that at 32 I wasn't exactly a 'kid'.

'Cocky he was too,' she continued. 'He asked a few things about you, but otherwise too keen on his own voice to worry that I might have told a white lie. He treated me like I was some weak little old woman.'

I thought about this for a moment. Carol had

been in initial shock at finding the body, but wasn't acting upset anymore. I didn't know what to read into that.

'So, you saw the body, came outside and rang 999, then saw us? That's what you told him?' I couldn't believe I was having to get my story straight to tell the police.

'Yes love, that's the one,' she said. 'To be honest, Edward, I'm hoping my part in all of this is over now. I feel sorry for the woman, god rest her soul, but this might not be the worst thing to happen around here.'

I didn't know what to think of that. Everyone reacts differently to death, but I'd seen a range of reactions to it in the last couple of hours. From Noah's naïve excitement to Kat's calm exterior and Dylan's practical, helpful reactions. And from Tim's arrogant, controlling responses to his daughter's smug indifference and subtly cruel jibes.

'Here we are,' Carol said as we reached the dining hall door. 'Just stick to what we said. You're only being spoken to as a witness, remember, not a suspect. Don't worry about the DC woman, she just sits there taking notes. But don't let that arrogant Inspector get the better of you.'

I walked into the dining hall. I don't know what I was expecting from a makeshift interview room, but I'd imagined more of a transformation to a police-like atmosphere. What I saw was a female Detective Constable sat at one of the dining tables with a pen and pad. Another officer, obviously the man that Carol disliked, was on the phone with his back to us.

'The Senior Investigating Officer won't be a minute,' she said politely.

As I sat waiting for him to finish the call, I could feel my mind leaving the room again, so much so I didn't see the SIO return and join us. I only noticed him when he sat back down and spoke.

'As if, Edward Crisp! This is a surprise.' I looked up to see a smug smile on the man's face, a face I recognised. It was Jamie Appleby, my old school bully.

16

'Are you sure you're okay on your own for this one, DI Appleby?'

'Of course, DC Gillespie. You get a break. It's only informal at this stage, and Edward's an old friend of mine.'

I was so lost in my thoughts that I barely noticed the female police officer smile as she left the room. I was 15 again. I was the last one left in the school dining hall, sat reading *A Murder is Announced* when the person I was most frightened of in the world cornered me.

'You think you're so much smarter than me, don't you?' the young bully had said. 'Sat reading your poncey murder mysteries. Let's see how much help Miss Marple is to you now.'

He grabbed the book, then pushed my arms away effortlessly as I tried to get it back. He sat down opposite me at the table with the book in his hand. He made me watch every second of what he did next, looking me in the eye the whole time as he tore every page from the book one by one.

I looked down in horror at the three hundred odd pages scattered across the table and floor.

'What a shame Crisp, you'll never find out who did it!' he gloated as he stood up to leave.

He turned back and came uncomfortably close to me so I could feel his breath on my ear. 'Nobody cares who did it. Get a life.'

And with that he turned and left, leaving me to gather the pieces I've been picking up ever since.

It was a new school building and a new dining hall, but the same two boys sat opposite each other at the table for the first time in sixteen years. But this time he was a Detective Inspector, and I was a suspect in his investigation. Maybe he would finally tell me who did it.

17

When you overthink everything as much as I do, sometimes the best thing to do with a problem is to stop focussing on it.

So, until that moment, sat at that table facing Jamie Appleby again, I had not allowed myself to relive our past. It had popped into my head briefly when I was thinking about Noah's situation with Gracie, but I had batted it straight back out of there.

Now that his colleague had left, I looked at him properly for the first time. He seemed to defy ageing – his dirty blonde hair looked salon fresh, and he still had the winning smile that had helped him become Head Boy. His popularity and success in school made his treatment of me seem even worse. He'd had everything he wanted; why did he do it?

If I'd allowed myself to think about him over the years, I probably would have imagined him as a smarmy City stockbroker or something along those lines. I knew he'd left Chalk Gap a long time ago, but I didn't know what had happened to him – funnily enough, I wasn't friends with him on social media.

Depending on your view of police officers, I wasn't sure he was up to the job. If you imagine the police to be fair, hard-working, brave upholders of the law then probably not. But if you're counting the corrupt, cruel, bullying versions often seen in the media, then he'd fit right in.

Either way, he had done exceptionally well to make Inspector already at our age; he must have been promoted rapidly in the last few years. I understand from the crime fiction I read that even getting into CID as a DC is hard for a young officer, let alone then making it to DS and DI.

Then it hit me. What the D in each of those stood for. *Detective* Constable, *Detective* Sergeant and now *Detective* Inspector. He was a detective. The thing I've always read about, the thing I used to dream of becoming, the thing he used to bully me for. If success was a poker game, he had seen the amateur detectives of my childhood dreams and raised it for a fully fledged Detective Inspector, in charge of his own team and investigating a murder at our old school. The school that I now worked.

And he had just asked his colleague to leave. They were both meant to interview me. What did he have planned? Time to find out.

'Edward bloody Crisp! Good to see you, mate.'

I eyed him suspiciously. 'Why did you ask your colleague to leave?'

'Mate, we've known each other for twenty years. We don't need her here. I don't know all the other witnesses. I remember that caretaker woman, but she had no clue who I was. It surprised me, cos she always was a nosy cow.'

He looked at me, expecting me to chat to him. I didn't.

'This is my first time back in Chalk Gap in a decade. My parents moved to Lewes years ago, and I had no other reason to come back here.' He paused, then added, 'I'm part of Sussex Police CID.'

I hadn't asked, but he seemed like he wanted to talk. I don't know where it came from, but I found myself saying something back to him.

'Sorry Jamie, I haven't got a copy of *A Murder Is Announced* on me today for you to rip up in my face.'

He stared at me, his expression changing. I thought I saw a flash of anger in his eyes, but it passed, and then he looked sad. He looked down at the table and didn't reply for a few moments.

'I might have gone a bit too far in school, mate.'

A bit too far? 'Oh, do you think?'

And then we talked. I haven't reported the conversation verbatim as I'm not sure I could remember it all, and I have a tendency for exaggeration when I'm emotionally involved in a story I'm telling.

But talked we did. He said he didn't know why he did it, but he knew it was wrong. He used going away to university as a chance to reinvent himself, to leave the cruel side of himself behind. He mentioned all the A*s he got for GCSEs and A Levels before that, and his university stories were peppered with the successes he had. There still seemed to be a sliver of arrogance in Jamie that he had always had. Despite seeming it, he hadn't even said the words *I'm sorry*.

Then I realised. He said he didn't know why he did it, but I did. Why does anybody bully? The man in front of me had very little self-esteem. I couldn't comprehend this. He had always had the looks, the ability, the personality. Success had always come easily to him, and his position in the police force at such a young age suggested that it still did.

If it seems from this that I said very little, that's correct. I congratulated him in all the right places, laughed politely at his university stories, and briefly answered his questions about what I'd been up to myself. But I hated every second.

And I was right to. This man had made my life hell. And he hadn't come especially to apologise, he had come to investigate a murder that I was caught up in.

I've kept our personal conversation and our conversation about the murder separate in my account here, because that's exactly what he did. After he had finished reminiscing, there was a pause and I saw his expression change again. I could almost see the box being ticked off on the list in his head – that he had carried out his apology (well, technically he hadn't), we had caught up a reasonable amount, and now it was time to get down to business.

He picked up his pen and emphasised turning a new page of his pad, as he explained that this was an informal conversation to establish the facts, and that a formal witness statement would be taken by his colleague later. The way he said it suggested he was too important for those kinds of trivialities.

'So, Edward Crisp. School librarian, been working here for... how long, mate?'

'Nine years.'

'Nine years,' he repeated for no reason. 'So, Mrs Fletcher tells me that when she found the body at about 8.15, she came outside and you were out there waiting.'

'That's right, yes. I mean, no.'

'Yes or no? Which do you mean?'

'I'm sorry. I mean, yes, I was outside. But no, I wasn't waiting. I was just arriving.'

He glanced at me suspiciously and again made a pantomime of looking down to write what I'd said. 'Right. And I understand you had a student with you, is that right?'

'Yes. Noah Oakley, my assistant librarian.' I imagined Noah sat here and thought of me at his age again. I considered Jamie for a moment. Even though I had no reason to think this version of Appleby would be cruel to Noah, something inside me said that I didn't want him to experience this. 'He has special educational needs.'

Jamie smiled, as if he'd read my mind. 'Don't worry, Edward mate, I know he's a minor. I don't have to speak to him for now, but if I need him, we will arrange it with his mother.'

I grimaced. I didn't particularly want Appleby talking to Emma either.

After that, the interview was quite routine. I confirmed what had happened (with the slight change I'd agreed with Carol) and it seemed to go alright. If he suspected that Carol or I had lied, he didn't show it. The interview seemed to be over and he put his pencil down and closed his notepad to show this.

'That's the interview part over, mate. My colleagues will take your statement later.'

'Thanks, Jamie – sorry, DI Appleby. And thanks for, you know, for before.' I was about to stand up to go.

'Just a sec, mate.' He seemed to expect this. 'Call me Jamie now, for starters. None of that DI crap – like I said, the proper part is over. But mate, come on. You've been at this school for years and lived in this village all your life. And I remember how much you loved those murder mysteries. You must have theories about what happened here.'

This was getting stranger. Now he was asking for *my* opinion about the case? Something didn't add up, and I decided not to take the bait. 'I've no idea. Reading murder mysteries doesn't qualify me to solve a case like this.'

'You're right, it doesn't.' He looked at me and paused before what he knew was his killer line.

'So why did you go and see the body?'

18

I never imagined that I'd be caught lying in a murder investigation, much less that Jamie Appleby would be the one to do it. The hot shot detective had just found a new number one suspect. The weirdo from his school days, now the lying, possibly murdering weirdo from his school days, Edward Crisp.

'It wasn't difficult to figure out, Edward. The CCTV might be gone, but the swipe card entry records aren't. Carol Fletcher swiped herself into the Executive offices at 7:57am, 15 minutes earlier than she told us she did. She rang 999 at 8:15am, around the time you told us you arrived. Earlier, you told me you had given yourself two hours to prepare the library before you were meant to be there at 10am.'

'Two hours, or thereabouts.'

'Come off it, mate – you were always so precise. All the years that have passed and you don't seem like you've changed much, no offence.' He was wrong about that.

'If the Edward I know says he had two hours to prepare, he means he had two hours to prepare. You arrived at 8am and you and that kid went to look at the body. I just need to know why you lied about it.'

I didn't like where this was going. I especially didn't like Noah being brought into it.

'Jamie, please leave Noah out of it.'

There was a pause while he thought. 'I'm on to something here. I understand he has an obsession for murder mysteries, doesn't he? Like you always did. And he has special educational needs, you said.'

'Yes, he does but I don't see what -'

'I didn't tell you the truth before, mate. When I said I didn't know why I bullied you. I did it because I felt threatened by you. And even more because I feared you. I was scared because I thought you were psycho.'

'Jamie, what is this? You apologised.' Even though technically he didn't.

'I know I did, mate. I meant it. But there's this kid, who seems very similar to how you were at his age. Obsessed with murder mysteries, hanging round outside the building. He could be involved.'

'You've got this all wrong!' This wasn't going well. I could feel myself starting to get angry.

'I've seen crimes committed by people with all sorts of conditions and disorders. Sounds harsh, mate, but it's a fact.' Just the word 'conditions' told me everything I needed to know. He hadn't grown up at all – no empathy or humanity. Maybe he was still the same judgemental bully he'd always been.

'Now you might be alright, but we don't know that this kid is,' he continued. 'We don't know that the murder wasn't just some game for his amusement.'

'This is ridiculous.' It was. I wouldn't expect a Detective Inspector to be correlating these things. The old Appleby was still in there.

'I bet it was his suggestion to see that body, wasn't it?'

I looked at the floor, not wanting to confirm this.

'I thought as much. I bet he imagines you and him can investigate the crimes?'

'What makes you think that?'

'Because that's what you would have done when you were his age.'

I sighed. I was still trying to work out whether or not Jamie was a good person. He seemed to be a good detective.

'Look, mate. I know you have good intentions, but you have to stay away. And make sure that kid does too. I've seen civilians go poking their nose round cases before and it never ends well.'

The word 'civilians' fired my anger.

'And if that kid has something to do with it, we will find out. But he will make it worse for himself if he gets involved in the investigation. You both will.'

I couldn't work out if this was a threat or not. A friendly warning, maybe?

But he hadn't finished. 'I also understand that the guy who's missing is your housemate too.' Another statement. Never a question. He seemed to know everything already.

'This murder happened at my workplace,' I replied. 'I know everyone on your suspect list.'

'You don't know who's on my suspect list. And I hope you don't have one of your own. This stuff is way out of your league, mate.'

He continued. 'There is something you're allowed to know though. There will be a warrant out for Patrick's arrest tomorrow, if he's not reappeared by then.'

So they thought it was Patrick. Was it because he ran away? Did they think the button belonged to him?

'I don't know what you think I know, but I want to know where he is just as much as you do.'

'Mate, I've done my homework. I know you followed him out of the school grounds yesterday. If you found him, then you might be the last person to see him.'

'Yes, I followed him.' There was no use lying. I told him about the beach yesterday afternoon and even showed him the text message Patrick had sent me.

'Sorry buddy I'm not going to make tonight. Cheers for finding me at the beach. Will explain everything soon.'

'So, this was sent at 9:12 pm,' Jamie said out loud to himself. 'He could have been to the school in that time, committed the murder and then got the hell out of town.'

'No, no way!' I said desperately. Then something occurred to me. 'You mentioned the swipe records a few minutes ago. What time did someone access the building last night?'

'That's for me to know, mate.'

'But if we know that, then it helps us work out who put the poison in there and when. We can rule out a lot of the suspects.'

'Edward, there is no "we." Mate, I will make this really clear.' He stood up and leaned forward over the desk. I had flashbacks to fifteen years ago as he spoke in a slow, deadly soft voice. 'Stay away from my investigation.'

This time I wasn't a silent victim. 'Jamie, I'm not going to let you put the blame on my best friend or one of my students.'

He glared at me as he returned to his seat, a flash of anger in his eyes again.

'You what, mate? You're not going to *let me*?'

'I can help you find the truth,' I said desperately.

I saw something flash across his face and I thought I was in for another threat, but it subsided. It seemed like DI Appleby was back, not school bully Jamie.

'I'm a police professional and you are a civilian who has already been found to be lying about the case. You could have tampered with evidence, I could arrest you right now if I wanted to. But I'm just warning you, for the last time, do not get involved with this case.'

As I left the dining hall, I knew one thing. I would definitely investigate this murder.

19

'We need to make a list of all our suspects and their motives.'

Noah and I were in the library. Carol had persuaded PC Wood to let us leave the staffroom and wait in the library as we had 'urgent work to finish.' As long as we didn't go near the crime scene, he'd reluctantly said this was allowed (not that she gave him much choice).

Noah had been delighted, to say the least, that we would look into things ourselves. He had immediately sourced flip chart paper, pens, highlighters and post-it notes – everything he thought would be useful for our 'investigation room.'

'Okay, Sir. So the list of suspects are all the people that had access to the room with the swipe cards. And this is the same list as the people in the building yesterday, plus me.'

He was certainly being very thorough and thought nothing of including himself on the list as he ran through it.

'I think we need to add Brian Fletcher to the list, he could have accessed Carol's keys.'

I realised I had used first name pronouns while he had been using Mr and Miss 'teacher names'. This wasn't a school project. I was taking this seriously. Noah and I knew about murder suspects and motives inside out, we had to prove that it wasn't Patrick. And I also had to prove to Appleby that it wasn't Noah.

'Sir, do you think this is a closed circle mystery or could it possibly be someone else?'

I wanted to keep Noah out of his fictional fantasy land; this was a real murder case. But he made a good point – did we know for certain that it could only be one of these people and not someone from outside the school?

'At the moment, I think it's likely that it is one of those people, yes Noah.' I was still struggling to believe that someone I knew was a murderer. But it was looking likely.

I next shared the list of questions I'd made in my head earlier with Noah. We attempted to answer them on flip-chart paper.

Who deleted the CCTV, was it the murderer?

Not known yet, it seems likely.

Was Miss Finch poisoned, and if so how?

Likely explanation is poison via the water dispenser or the disposable cup she drank from. We don't know what kind of poison or where it came from. We need to find out!

How long had she been dead and when did the poisoning take place?

Again, we don't know. The police will have this information soon. Are they likely to share it with the school (Kat or Tim?)? How can we find out?

Who did the button belong to and was it related to her murder?

It looks like a button from a man's shirt. Yesterday, most staff were dressed down as the school wasn't open. Tim Hunt was the only person who wore a shirt. Could it be him? How long had the button been there? It must have only been since yesterday – Carol is a thorough cleaner, Miss Finch would also have noticed it if longer. Must be Tim, another visitor we haven't accounted for or the murderer's.

I looked over our list. It didn't seem like we knew much, and there weren't many ways to find out.

Appleby had warned me not to interfere again, so it's not like I could call and ask him.

'The swipe records,' Noah suddenly piped up. 'You said DI Appleby wouldn't tell you, but I bet someone in the school could, like Mrs Fletcher.'

He was right. The police already knew this and were sitting on a useful piece of information. They must surely know who accessed the school out of hours and at what time. Did that mean it was Patrick, as Appleby's suspicions seemed to be centred around him? Or perhaps there was no record of anyone coming into the school last night, so it must have been during the day? We had to find this out. We had our next step.

20

Our 'next step' was foiled almost immediately. Carol said she wasn't allowed into her office; they had already closed the room off to preserve evidence. Even knowing the PC's mother as long as she had, I doubt he would be persuaded to steal evidence for her.

Noah and I were now walking the seafront route back to his mum's café. I'd decided to walk him home and have a word with her, to explain what was going on. He'd spent most of the morning hurriedly typing away 'case notes' (his term, not mine) in his phone, and now the battery had died before he'd even used it to tell her what was going on.

As we walked along the seafront path towards the village centre, the lazy mid-afternoon sun reminded me of taking the same walk about this time yesterday in search of Patrick. There was no barbecue smell this time, although the seagulls were still out in force in search of any food left by sunbathers. Perhaps they knew that their main tormentor had done a runner.

As Noah spoke, he addressed the concerns going around my brain. 'It won't be Mr Herrera, Sir. The missing suspect is way too obvious.'

I had rolled my eyes without realising. I hoped he hadn't seen. I was trying to steer Noah away from relying on his beloved murder mystery tropes. Although I'd give anything now to be taking in the adventures of Hercule Poirot or Lord Peter Wimsey rather than living an apparent real-life version.

'Major suspect going missing is such a cliché, Sir! So it can't be him. He will have an unrelated secret. And it's never the obvious suspect anyway.'

'There are plenty of stories where it *is* the obvious suspect. We just get a double bluff so we think it's too obvious, or they're eliminated from the enquiry and then it was them all along.' I couldn't believe I was playing along with this.

'Hm.... Maybe, Sir. But that means he will be back soon, and we will accidentally eliminate him later anyway. Either way, we don't have to worry about him for now.'

'Noah...' I stopped myself to think about my wording. He meant well, and obviously this was just his way of seeing the world. 'Mr Herrera is my friend and I'm worried about him. I don't think he did it, but I'm worried that the police do and he'll still be in trouble.'

'Don't worry, Sir. We will find out who did it! We have to remember though, murder mysteries always have surprises. It won't be as straightforward as we think.'

'How do you mean?' I knew I would regret asking this.

'Well, it could be anything. Maybe she wasn't dead the first time, and she was in on it with Miss Fletcher to trick us for some reason. But Miss Fletcher double crossed her somehow and killed her for real afterwards.'

'That's ridiculous!'

'Or maybe everybody did it. They were all in on it together, and they conspired to kill her and cover their tracks. The police will never pin it on any of them, so it's a perfect crime.'

I glanced across at the beach where a family barbecue was taking place. There must have been about a dozen people sat there – the same amount who conspired together in Agatha Christie's probably most famous mystery. I imagined the entire staff body (who hadn't included me) all plotting together to poison Finch. 'I don't think so, Noah.'

'Or maybe I did it.'

Wait, what?

'The other most famous twist. The sidekick who everyone thinks is helping the detective, is really the killer all along.'

'Well, that trope is specifically the narrator.' Then I realised he had been typing away in his notes app on his phone all day. I meant it when I told you the narrator didn't do it, but I only meant in my version of the story.

'Only joking, Sir!' He laughed loudly and awkwardly. 'It's none of those things. It will be a big twist we haven't thought of. Wait 'til you read my novella – it's got a twist that's never ever been done. But...'

This was when something strange happened. For the first time since the murder, Noah went quiet. He looked worried.

'Sir, people won't think it's me, will they?'

This was something both Appleby and Carol had already mentioned. But I wasn't going to tell him that. 'Why would you say that, Noah?'

'Just because I like murder mysteries so much.' This was the first time I'd ever heard him talk about this subject without enthusiasm.

'So do I, Noah. And I had access to the school – you didn't.'

'And I said it would happen then it did. But it was nothing to do with me.'

It surprised me he was worrying about this, but at least he was separating reality from his fictional world. I needed to reassure him. 'Of course it wasn't. You told me all about your prediction and I know you didn't do it. You wouldn't have told me the day before if you were planning a murder, would you?'

'No, I suppose I wouldn't,' he said with relief in his voice. I cheered him up by playing detective again.

'Noah, starting from tomorrow, we need to interview each suspect.' I knew he'd love this. 'Find out their motives, their whereabouts, see if we can spot any of them lying.'

'Oh everyone lies, remember. We just have to work out if they're lying about the murder.'

Another mystery trope. Almost every investigation is blurred by innocent people lying in their interviews to cover up another secret that wasn't the murder. I allowed a smile to shape my face. I'd just done it myself to Appleby. Maybe Noah's mystery tropes were closer to the truth than I'd thought.

'Agreed. And we must take different tactics with each of them. A couple of suspects we can just openly talk to, but for some of them we'll have to think about how to do it. Tim Hunt would be on to his DCI friend in no time if he thought I was interfering with the investigation.'

This led me to tell him something I'd given a lot of thought to. If I was taking this seriously, I couldn't have Noah present at the investigations. But I didn't want to hurt his feelings.

'We need to work together cleverly on this, Noah,' I started. 'I don't think the suspects will be as open with us if a student is there. But you're a crucial part of the investigation.'

'But I won't be in the interviews?' He stopped in his tracks and looked straight at me.

'No, but this is the clever bit. The suspects won't know, but secretly you've written the interview questions – really clever ones to trip them up. And because I'm their friend and colleague, they'll trust me and won't suspect anything.'

'Yes! Mr Crisp, that's genius!' He shook his hands wildly through the air in excitement. 'So it will be like I'm in the interviews but they won't know I am?'

'Exactly.' My plan had worked. 'Besides, Poirot always gave Hastings secret side missions to complete without him.'

'I'm so excited, Sir! I can't wait for tomorrow!' He almost jumped for joy. 'I think I'm going to watch some old *Poirot* episodes tonight to remember some tips for interviewing.' At least his mention of the TV show assured me he still knew that fictional detectives were just that.

As we arrived at the café, I could see a handful of people sat outside with Emma collecting at the tables. *Wave* café was in a great location, with a terrace directly on the seafront and the café itself just opposite, across the seafront path. It wasn't somewhere I'd been much, despite it being on the same square as my family's pub. I have my set breakfast routine each morning (orange juice, two slices of buttered toast) and I don't like hot drinks, so I've never had much reason to go. Maybe that was something that needed to change when this was over. I'd enjoyed chatting to Emma the previous night.

'Oh hello, you two! Noah, thank god, you're alright!'

She ran over when she saw us, almost dropping the cups she was collecting. She threw her arms around her son and hugged him tightly, looking at me as she did so.

'Edward, thank you so much for bringing him home. I heard about the murder but couldn't get hold of him.' She turned her attention to her son, who was getting crushed between her arms and her body. 'Noah, you didn't even tell me you were going to school today! What happened to your phone?'

'My battery died, mum. Get off me!' He tried to wriggle from her grasp.

'I'm sorry, I know you hate that. I was just worried!'

Reassured, she let him go while Noah brushed himself down. 'I'm sorry, Mum, I just needed my phone for important evidence.' I realised that this was the first time I'd seen the two of them together.

'Let's go inside and I'll get you two a drink,' Emma said.

'Mum, have you got your portable charger in there?' Noah asked, pointing to the large front pouch in her apron. 'I want to have a walk on the beach and ask witnesses what they know about Miss Finch.'

'Okay then,' she agreed, handing him the phone charger. 'But don't go too far and make sure you're polite.'

As Noah skipped off we headed inside the café. I realised immediately that I couldn't have been inside since Emma had taken it over. I would have remembered. Every wall was painted bright fluorescent green. That would be noticeable in itself, but the gaudy colour was host to a series of beach-themed cartoon murals – children building sandcastles, a pier, giant seagulls escaping with food (Patrick would love that one) and men and women of various shapes and sizes posing in swimming costumes, some wearing knotted handkerchiefs on their head – one even had a 'kiss me quick' hat. This was a classic British seaside heaven (or hell, depending on your perspective).

'They're awful, aren't they?' Emma said as she laughed. I didn't know what to say. Anything that goes beyond expected social responses leaves me struggling to find the correct response. She seemed to sense this.

'It's okay, they're meant to be awful!' she continued quickly. 'My dad took me to Blackpool when I was little and this old British seaside stuff is what I remember most. As soon as I got the lease for the café, I knew what I wanted to do with it.'

My eyes strayed further to a shelf near the till point, filled with books, but I couldn't see what they were from where we stood.

'Go have a look,' she said from behind me. 'I admit I stole the idea from the pub anyway.'

'It's great,' I replied as I strolled over. 'The more public places that have books to read, the better.' It's true – one reason I did the book corner in the pub was to increase reading habits in the village. Our village library had been closed for years and we had to go to Eastbourne or Seaford, while our only other access to books was the stock in the village charity shop. I glanced at the range of modern psychological thrillers with 'girl' in the title and women in windows, along with several brightly coloured rom coms.

'It's not as good as your collection in the pub,' Emma said with a slightly red face as she picked up her teacup and sipped from it.

Even though I'd defended Christie passionately earlier, I hated snobbery about modern genre fiction and she wouldn't find it from me. 'Reading is reading,' I said, and I meant it. 'The pub collection isn't all Golden Age stuff, there's loads of great modern crime novels.' I thought of my own bookshelves at home, with hundreds of mysteries and detective novels from every decade. And Kat on my case to put at least some of them in the attic and make some space in the house. But my mind wandered to the book that wasn't amongst them, the one that should have been but never made it.

I didn't realise how long I was staring at the books in silence until I felt Emma's hand on my shoulder. 'Tell me what you're thinking,' she said softly.

Miss Finch had been murdered. That should have been my focus. And it was. But becoming involved in the real life mystery along with the conversation about books had stirred a memory.

'*Ten Green Bottles*,' I said out loud finally, before repeating it. '*Ten Green Bottles*.'

'What's that?'

Ten Green Bottles was meant to be my debut novel, my masterpiece, my homage to Golden Age detective fiction. I wrote it across three different summers while I was at university, a product of a long love of classic murder mysteries since childhood. Using the classic Agatha Christie trope of a nursery rhyme title, it was my modern answer to vintage crime novels.

'Why didn't you publish it?' Emma asked as she took my hand and led me to sit at the nearest table.

The pain of the memory stopped me from speaking for a moment. Filled with the confidence and inspiration from an English Literature degree, I was convinced I'd written a bestseller. I'd made it out of my village four days a week for three entire years. I knew everything there was to know about Literature all over the world. I was leaving with First Class Honours. Hell, I'd even found a best friend. I felt like I could do anything. I was unstoppable. Or so I thought.

'I couldn't get an agent for it. Eventually, I stopped trying.' I meant to keep my continuing thoughts in my head but before I knew it I was saying them out loud. 'I remember the year after I graduated, crossing each agent off in my *Writers & Artists Yearbook* when the rejection letters came in. I'd started at the school library, but I thought it would only be temporary for a few months until my writing career took off. There were a few agents left to hear from. It was only when I came back to work for my second academic year after summer I realised – they weren't going to reply.'

'Edward, that's awful. But it's not too late. Forget those stuffy publishing houses. Publishing independently is massive now – you could be a huge success.'

My mind was lost in the missed opportunities of the past. 'Indie publishing hadn't taken off by then, it was nearly a decade ago.'

'But you could now?'

This was something Mum was regularly saying to me and I had my answer ready. 'I could. But I just got used to being a librarian.' I looked at her, before sounding as convincing as I could. 'I love my job and I love this village, I've got everything I need. I'm happy.'

She looked back at me and smiled. Did she believe me? 'As long as you are, that's the main thing.'

'Besides,' I replied, changing the subject, 'it looks like we have a real life mystery on our hands now.'

'A murder in our village, who'd have thought it?' I could see the worry on her face and I knew what she was going to ask next. 'Tell me honestly, how's Noah's coped with it?'

I didn't know how much detail to go into. I had let her murder-obsessed son sneak into a crime scene after all. I decided it was best to let him give her the details. 'Just how you saw him outside, thinking we are in a murder mystery. For want of a better term, he seems to be enjoying it.'

She thought about this as she sipped her tea. 'Oh Edward, what must people think! I didn't even know he was going to that blasted school today.' I felt the heavy thump of the cup on the table as she clanked it down. 'I love my son so much but I worry about him. What people say, that he doesn't behave normally.'

She seemed like she wanted to talk, so I smiled at her as a cue to continue.

'I've never minded the murder mystery thing. He discovered them through me taking him to the library every week. I just didn't think he'd become so obsessed with it.' She fiddled with the handle of her teacup as she paused, before continuing with a new determination. 'But look how happy it makes him. There's an entire world of fictional stories that help our world make sense to him. If this is his way of coping, then I don't mind, and to hell with what people think. Besides,' she smiled, 'it seems like you guys are doing your own investigation?'

Maybe she wouldn't like this. Having an obsession with fiction is one thing, getting involved in real life murder cases is quite another.

'It's okay, I think it's great - he's having the time of his life out there,' she smiled again. 'I can imagine what other kids say about his murder stuff, but he doesn't care so neither should I.'

I was trying to work out how to reply and whether to mention Gracie, when I felt my phone vibrate in my pocket. I looked and it was Kat.

'I've found something out,' she declared without even saying hello. 'It turns out Tim wasn't exaggerating after all about being mates with the DCI. He rang him up and you'll never guess what he found out.'

'Go on.'

'As we thought, looks like it was poison. But the thing is, we also found out where it came from. Annoyingly, Gracie's guess was right. Miss Finch was poisoned with Carol's insecticide for the school garden – it contained cyanide.'

21

After leaving the café, I headed across the village square to the Chalk Head. I decided that being in such close proximity (although the whole of our village is in close proximity by default), I'd pop into the pub and see my family. Mum would appreciate it; I'd had four missed calls from her throughout the day, and I knew she'd be dying to hear the gossip.

As I glanced back at the café with the pebbled beach and waves behind it, I juggled pleasant thoughts of Emma with anxious ones about the investigation. I knew that the use of school ID was already quite certain, but this fresh information about the poison confirmed it – this was someone who knew the school.

Kat told me that the school may be in trouble for even having the insecticide on the premises. Sodium cyanide apparently hadn't been used as insecticide for many years, and it seemed that Carol's bottle of it dated back many years. Carol had been at the school for over twenty years, but she even could have inherited it from the caretaker before her. She'd obviously just moved her entire stock over to the new school without going through it. Luckily for her, Miss Finch was no longer around to punish her for such an oversight.

I walked in to see the pub empty, except for my mum behind the bar and my dad sat at it on the customer side.

'Here he is!' he shouted cheerfully, giving me the same greeting he did every time he saw me.

'Never mind that," Mum interrupted. "I've been ringing you! Edward love, I've been worried. The murderer didn't get you then?'

'Yes they did love, he's a ghost, can't you tell?' my dad remarked, before laughing away at his own joke (I think it was a joke).

'I just can't believe it,' she continued. 'I said to your dad, a murder in our village… I honestly just can't believe it!'

'What do you think happened then?' my dad asked.

I sat down at the bar and gave them a potted version of my day.

Mum immediately defended Carol following the latest revelation. 'I've known Carol for years, there's no way she's a poisoner.'

I didn't think so either; it would have been very

easy for someone to access her cupboard and get what they needed. Someone like her husband?

'I also heard who the bloody police officer was.'

How had mum found that out so quickly?

'That Jamie Appleby has got a cheek popping up in Chalk Gap again after what he did to you, he'd better not show his face round here!'

'It's alright, mum. He apologised actually.'

'Did he now? Well, I doubt he meant it. He was probably pretending to be nice so he could get whatever information he wanted out of you.'

This was a theory I'd had myself.

'Anyway, never mind him!' she continued. 'Who do you think did it? I reckon it was that flash b word with the Mercedes.'

I grinned to myself. I knew Tim Hunt would be her number one suspect. Mum doesn't really do subtlety. If she was a mystery writer, she'd make it the nastiest, smarmiest person every time.

'And no one's seen his wife for years! She apparently ran off, but what if he killed her as well?'

'Mum!' In her mind, Tim was now a full-on serial killer.

'I wonder what'll happen to his daughter if he's guilty?' she mused.

'Technically, Gracie is a suspect herself,' I informed her. 'She was in school with her dad yesterday and she has an access card.'

'Is she now?' It delighted Mum to have a fresh piece of news. 'Hmmm, I doubt it's her. Mind you, with the upbringing she's had from him, you never know.'

'Brian Fletcher's got to be a top suspect.' My dad chipped in. 'The state of him last night. And it's no secret what he thought of that Miss Finch.'

'Yes, he could easily have got hold of Carol's keys,' my mum added.

Mum and dad were clearly enjoying themselves. To them, this was the gossip of the day – like a real life soap opera unfolding in their village, with new instalments to catch up on all the time.

'Remember this is a murder case, mum. Carol was really upset this morning.'

'Of course she was, why else do you think I was getting in touch with her?' To find out the gossip, I thought. 'You're as bad as your brother, you know! He's been in a mood all day, telling me to mind my own business!'

'Why's he so bothered?' I asked.

'Oh, I don't know, probably being overprotective of you, as usual. He doesn't see how brave you are. I told him, Edward's going to solve the murder!'

I laughed and told her about my plan to do my own investigation to help clear Patrick's name.

'It's definitely not Patrick!' Mum had always had a soft spot for him. 'No way will a nice lad like him have anything to do with it. There'll be a good reason he's disappeared. Maybe one of his relatives in Spain has taken ill or something.'

'Hold up, look who's here!' My dad whispered, nudging my mum.

Brian Fletcher came through the door looking sheepish. His shirt looked ironed for the first time I could remember, and he was wearing his blue suit jacket I hadn't seen since he was last in school. He seemed to be going for damage control.

'Linda, Casper, I want to apologise for last night,' he shouted as he walked from the door, his words arriving before he did. 'Pass on my apologies to Alfie too. You'll get no more trouble from me in here.'

'I guess your reason for trouble has gone now,' Dad said.

'Casper!' my mum told him off.

'No, Linda, that's fair,' Brian said. 'But Finch is still causing me trouble after she's gone. Me and Carol have just had a row about it.'

'Oh, I'm sorry to hear that,' my mum said. She didn't seem it.

'Actually, Edward, I was hoping to catch you. I believe you were with my Carol when she found the body. I wanted to say thank you and buy you a drink. Can we have a chat somewhere quiet?' He gestured across the pub.

'Of course, Brian, you two sit down, I'll bring them over.' Mum was eager for fresh gossip.

'Cheeky pig,' I heard her say as we walked away. 'Does he think we're going to listen in?'

'I mean it, Edward. Thanks for being there with Carol today. It was a nasty shock for her,' Brian said as we sat down.

'How is she now?'

He laughed before responding. 'Back to normal, nagging me as usual.'

'I hope she's okay. It's been a shock for everybody, but finding the body makes it worse for her.'

'She told me you saw the body too,' he said.

I flinched. I hoped that would stay between us.

'It's okay, I think it's a good thing you nosing into what happened.' Using the word 'nosing' didn't suggest this was true, but never mind.

'Better than that cocky twerp Appleby investigating.'

Of course. Brian used to teach both me and

Jamie, he'd been at the school that long.

'Carol didn't even recognise him, she never had much to do with him at school and he's not been in the village for years. Was only when she said his name and described him, I realised.'

The mention of Appleby unsettled me. 'Small world,' I offered.

'How was he with you then? He used to give you a hard time, didn't he?'

I considered how to answer. Was I speaking to a man I'd known two thirds of my life, a colleague and my old teacher? Or a murder suspect? I decided to be honest but brief.

'He was okay with me, actually. He apologised for the old days, he didn't seem keen on me investigating though.'

'I bet he didn't! Take no notice. I was wondering, did he, erm... did he say anything about who he suspected?'

I told him briefly about Patrick.

'Bloody idiot, of course it's not Patrick. Typical of him to get the wrong person. All mouth, no trousers.'

'To be honest, Brian, I'm worried about him blaming Patrick too.'

'Not just Patrick, he could blame any of us. I'm not sure about Noah, you know. Carol told me he was on the scene, there's always been something -' he cut off. Mum was at our table with the drinks.

'Don't mind me boys, I'm not listening!' she insisted. She even put her fingers in her ears as she walked away, singing 'la, la, la.'

'The thing is, Edward...' He paused as he was considering what he would say. 'The thing is, I'm worried Appleby's gonna fit me up for this.'

'He always hated me when I taught him, and I suppose... well, I suppose I made his life difficult too. I could tell how cocky he was, and I saw what he was like with you. I wanted him to know there was one teacher who could see through his sparkling Head Boy routine.'

'It was a long time ago, Brian. He was quite fair with me.' Was he? I thought about what he'd said after the formal interview and his warning.

'Carol didn't see you again to tell you, but he called her back a second time. Was asking loads of questions about me, whether I'd have been able to access her keys and ID. He even knew about what happened here last night. Think he'd sent some of his bobbies into the village to ask questions. Dunno who'd have told him that though.'

I glanced at Mum and she looked away quickly, the picture of innocence. This was something she'd forgotten to mention.

'Me and Carol just got into a big argument about

it. She thinks it's my fault. I've got to get Appleby off my case.' He paused and looked at me, so intensely close that I looked away. 'I didn't do it, Edward.'

This was my first sit-down with a 'suspect' since I'd decided to investigate. And here he was pleading his innocence. Of course he was going to do that. I remembered what I'd told myself: *your friends and colleagues will lie to you during this*. I tried to forget the man I'd known all these years and imagine a dubious suspect I'd never met before today.

'I know I will be number one suspect for a lot of people,' he continued after downing half of his pint. 'Especially after my behaviour the last few weeks.' I could see mum at the bar rolling her eyes.

I decided to play good cop for now. 'Getting drunk and shouting about her doesn't make you a murderer, Brian.'

'Exactly, that's what I told Carol!' the enthusiasm in his voice told me my tactic was working. He had to feel comfortable talking to me if I was going to find out anything worthwhile. 'I mean, I know I made threats about her a couple of times.'

We were getting somewhere. 'Go on.'

'I gave half of my life to that school. It was my home.' He stared into his half-drunk pint. 'And just like that, that witch took it away from me. And don't tell me about speaking ill of the dead, I don't care.'

Brian's feelings for Finch were clear. And this was him sober. Drunk Brian could have turned these feelings into actions. I could feel his eyes on me, waiting for a response to his last comment.

'I wasn't going to, but you need to be careful what you say about her, Brian.'

'I suppose so, I don't want people thinking it's me. Anyway, I thought that was where you could help.'

'What can I do?'

'Well, you're looking into it, aren't you? You need to prove I didn't do it.'

I thought about what he'd said in the last few minutes. Did I believe him? I wasn't sure. But either way, I couldn't be promising to prove him innocent at this stage.

'Why should I believe you?' I said before I could stop myself.

'Bloody hell, Edward! How many years have I known you and your family? I even taught you.'

I felt a pang of guilt. 'You're right, I'm sorry.'

He stood up. 'No, I'm not having it. You think I'm gonna be the scapegoat, don't you? Well, I'm not having it.'

'Come on Brian, I didn't mean -'

'And I know it was you who told them about last night, Linda!' He shouted over to my mum.

'Now, hang on a second, Brian!' My mum wouldn't stand for this.

'I see. The whole Crisp family is closing ranks. Trying to put it on me!'

'Brian, calm down...' My dad stood up to walk over to our table.

'I was gonna get you to help me. Well do you know what? I don't need it. There's something I was gonna keep to myself, but why should I? Let's see if the police still think it was me once I've had a little chat with them!' And with that he walked out of the pub.

'What was all that about?' My dad wondered out loud.

'The cheek of him!' My mum raged. 'All the help we've given him, turning a blind eye when he gets drunk. I'm going to tell your brother he's barred! He's not coming in here again!'

I could hear my dad trying to calm her down, but my mind drifted as I tried to decipher Brian's last statement. What was he talking about? What had he been keeping to himself?

I didn't get much time to think as my phone rang. It was Patrick. Finally.

'Hello?' I answered, not knowing what to expect.

The line was silent; I thought he wasn't going to speak at first.

'Hello?' I asked again. I could hear the wind wherever he was.

'Edward,' he replied. 'Can you come and meet me, buddy?'

'Patrick, thank god you're back! Where have you been?'

'I just need you to come and meet me,' he said again. 'On your own.'

'Where are you?'

'I'm at the top of West Chalk Cliff.'

'Are you serious?' I ignored my rising panic and went straight into my instincts. 'Patrick, I'm on the way. Don't do anything stupid.'

22

I tried to get him to stay on the line, but he kept hanging up on me and now I was getting diverted every time. Which was probably just as well, as I could barely breathe as I climbed the steep slope which led to the top of West Chalk Cliff.

Unlike nearby Beachy Head or Birling Gap, there was no road or access by car to our West and East cliff tops; our village was on a flat road off the A259 until you came to our high street and Chalk Gap square. Your options for getting to the top were gradually climbing up the fields which lay either side of our village, or going up the unforgiving climb from the square like I was now.

It had taken everything to stop my dad coming with me, and my mum from phoning the police.

As I reached the top, the early evening August sky was still bright and allowed me to see perfectly. This wasn't some mad decision made in the dead of night at least. And he *had* called me.

I saw him straight away, sat far too close to the cliff edge for my liking. As I ran towards him and called his name, it was strange that I didn't notice the smell. It was only as I got to him, I realised. He was doing another barbecue.

'Patrick, what the hell? I've been going out of my mind! And this...' I could barely find the words through fury. 'I thought you were going to jump and all the time you were having a barbecue?' There might have been an f word in there I haven't included.

He looked at me, and I could see the sadness on his face. This thawed me a little. 'Where have you been, anyway?'

'Sit down, buddy,' he offered. 'I'm sorry.'

I sat down begrudgingly. 'I don't want any of your stupid burgers this time though.'

I looked at him in what was meant to be anger, but as soon as our eyes met we both started laughing.

'I'm sorry Edward, I would never jump. I didn't even think of it looking like that. I should have remembered your flair for the dramatic.'

'My flair for the dramatic? Says the guy who has been AWOL for 24 hours in the middle of a murder case.'

'Yeah, my bad,' he said. 'I can explain all of that.'

'I think you'd better,' I replied. 'Where have you been?'

'Driving,' he said. I wondered if he would elaborate or not, but then he launched into what he wanted to say. 'I packed a bag. I was going to leave and never come back. I drove round for hours, ended up the other side of London at first. I didn't know where to go. And then I went to Heathrow Airport.'

'You know Gatwick is less than an hour from here, don't you? And you call me dramatic.'

'I'm telling this in the wrong order,' he said. 'Well, the right order actually. But you should know buddy, I didn't even know Miss Finch was dead then. I turned my phone off for hours in the airport so no one could talk me out of it. When I turned it on and saw your message, I realised what it looked like. So I came back.'

This was his story, but I needed to be sure of all the facts. 'When did you leave?'

'About five in the morning. I think I accidentally took some shoes of yours too – sorry.'

Of course – that's where my shoes went. I ignored this and carried on with my questions. 'So why did you go? What could be so bad that you would leave Chalk Gap?'

'I've always told you I'm Spanish.' He looked out across the English Channel, as if Spain was the first country at the edge of the horizon.

'But you're not, is that it?'

'I am. My dad was Spanish, and I lived in Madrid from when I was three 'til we came here when I was 11. But my mum is actually Argentinian, and I was born there.'

'So?' I think I knew where this was going.

'I have an Argentinian passport and my parents never sorted it out, so I'm an Argentinian citizen, not a Spanish one. Which was fine when I was a kid, but not now.'

'How does that work? You've been in Europe for over 30 years.'

'When I turned 18, we tried to sort it out, but they gave me a 5 year student visa. When I qualified as a teacher and got this job, I got a 5 year work visa, then got a 2 year extension.'

'So that takes us to...' I was trying to do the maths quickly in my head.

'Last year. I spoke to Terry about it expiring soon, and he didn't seem to worry too much.'

I sighed. Terry was a fantastic Head but not the most organised person.

"So you're not legally in the country?' I was shocked at this. 'No wonder you were going to leave.'

'No, that's all fine. After Terry told me not to worry about work, I started looking into it and found out I could get UK right to remain as I've been here for 20 years.'

'So, it's all alright?'

'Well, the visa part is. My teacher contract was specifically linked to my work visa, so the contract expired with it. They could have let me go anytime in the last year. And Terry had said it was nothing to worry about. But-'

'- with Miss Finch it was something to worry about,' I finished for him. 'But surely she didn't want to fire you? She'd already got rid of Brian.'

'I don't know, buddy.' He looked weary. 'She called and grilled me on the expired work visa, so I told her about my right to remain. I thought it was all alright, but she called me in again the day after and told me I didn't have a valid contract and she could give me notice anytime.'

'Then what happened?'

'She said she understood I was popular and a skilled teacher, but that she saw through it. Said my personality is too big, I'm too friendly with students, I'm a show off.'

'But all that's rubbish. Your English results are always amazing, everyone knows you're a brilliant teacher. She couldn't have got rid of you, she had no good reason.'

'I had no contract remember, she didn't need one. It felt like she was torn between keeping a good member of staff and the fact that she just couldn't stand me.'

I felt bad for Patrick. This was so stupid; Miss Finch had been throwing her weight around for no reason. Brian I could understand, but she'd have been mad to get rid of Patrick.

'Did she try to get rid of you then?'

'No, she kept telling me she could if she wanted to. At first she used it to tell me to meet her standards – she thought I was slacking. Said that English at the school was good, but it had to be outstanding. She said she wanted me to be the first one in the building at 7.30am and the last one out twelve hours later.'

I nodded as I realised. She could do what she wanted.

'So I did all those things. I didn't mind, it's less work to do at home. I did everything she asked. But that wasn't the end. She started asking me for more unreasonable things - putting on loads of extra sports clubs, doing the school website, doing extra work in the other schools of the academy chain. I was trying to do it all at first, but just before the summer holidays it got too much.'

'So what did you do?' I felt my phone going in my pocket. It could wait.

'I told her I wasn't going to do it anymore. But she called my bluff and said she'd have Dylan make up the paperwork to give me notice to finish at the end of August.'

'She couldn't have got away with that. No one can blackmail you into doing loads of extra stuff you're not paid to do. I'm surprised you didn't tell her to shove it.'

'Edward, you know I love this job. And this village. She wasn't stupid, giving an English teacher notice in the middle of July? All the jobs for September are long gone by then. I'd have been unemployed or in supply teacher hell.'

'Yes, but, I mean what she was doing was unfair. You could have reported it.' I could feel my phone vibrating again, but this was more important.

'To who? I thought I'd try Tim first. He sided with her, quoted the "any other reasonable duties" thing in the contract.'

'But it's not reasonable!'

'I know that! He told me he'd have a word with her and get her to leave off.'

'And did she?'

'No. She called me in the next day and roasted me for going to Tim. It was the last day of term by then, last day in the old building. She said I better think about my attitude when we return if I want to stay at the school.'

'So what happened yesterday? You weren't exactly falling in line, coming in late and making a big entrance like that.'

'I did that on purpose. I thought about it loads over the summer and I decided I couldn't put up with it anymore. I thought, worst comes to worst, I can get another job.'

'You could have told me, Patrick. We drink together every Friday night. Or at the beach yesterday when I found you.'

'I just thought I'd deal with it myself,' he said sheepishly. I felt like something didn't add up somehow.

'But it didn't work, she was worse than ever to you yesterday.'

'I know, buddy. I just couldn't hack it. That's why I got out of there.'

'Were you actually going to leave over it?' I asked. 'Like you said, you could have just got another job.'

'It all got to me. She humiliated me, man. I'd spent all of summer worrying about it, and you know me – I don't worry about anything. I just got it in my head that things would never get better as long as I was at that school.'

'But you were going to leave the country?'

'I just thought I needed to get out and spend time with my family.'

'But your mum is here?'

'The rest of my family, I mean. I never would have gone. It was just a mad moment. But you must believe me, Edward, I didn't kill her.'

I laughed hearing those words. This was my best friend. 'Of course you didn't, I always knew that.'

We sat and chatted a little more, eating burgers from the barbecue (I gave in after all). I brought him up to speed with everything else in the investigation, and he said he would go straight to the police to explain where he'd been. As the sun set, I felt relieved but guilty for doubting him.

As we packed away the barbecue, I heard a voice shouting my name.

I looked up and saw my dad at the top of the slope, running towards us and panting. 'Edward, Edward, we need you!'

'Dad, what are you doing here? What's the matter?' This must have been the source of the calls.

'It's your brother. The police just arrested him for Miss Finch's murder.'

23

'It's not right! Edward, it's not right!' Mum paced up and down the pub floor for what must have been the two-hundredth time. To say she was panicking was an understatement. 'Don't just sit there, Casper. Do something, for god's sake!'

'I already told you, love, he could be there for hours, there's no point going there and just waiting. Edward can keep trying his detective friend.'

'Friend? It's that bully who's to blame for this. He's only done it to get at Edward. The way all those officers came in with their warrant, ransacking our flat, it's disgusting!'

It had been over an hour since Dad had found me, and this had been the scene since I'd arrived at the pub. I was almost grateful for mum's hysteria; it gave me something to focus on. Helping dad keep her calm was preventing me from falling into a similar state.

It just made no sense. Everything had pointed to it being one of our main group of suspects. Finding out that it was someone unconnected to

Miss Finch, let alone my brother, just didn't add up.

I stopped myself mid-thought. Unconnected to Miss Finch, *as far as we know*. If I wanted to get to the bottom of this, I would have to think like a detective and not someone with personal connections to the suspects.

How would Hercule Poirot have reacted if they had arrested Miss Lemon or Hastings for the murder? He would have used his "little grey cells" to solve the mystery objectively, even if they ended up being the murderer. Which would never happen. Would it?

No. For as much as I was convinced it couldn't be Patrick or Noah, I was doubly sure it wasn't my brother – my own flesh and blood.

But how much do adult siblings know about each other once they've grown up? I considered what I knew about Alfie Crisp, the person. Hard-working pub landlord, openly gay, patience of a saint with my mum and dad. I thought back to last night – and how kind he was coming to get me out of the toilets after my anxiety attack.

I was sure that my brother was innocent. But I couldn't keep thinking that about everyone who came under suspicion.

Was Patrick even in the clear? I'd remembered Finch saying in the meeting she saw him yesterday, but that didn't figure in Patrick's story.

He was still hiding something.

But I would come on to the other suspects tomorrow and do my best to find out who was guilty. For today, I had to find out why they had arrested my brother, and what his connection to the murder was.

It was at that moment something occurred to me. I knew why Alfie had been arrested. It made little sense at all, but I knew why.

'Dad, I'm just going to pop out to clear my head a bit. Tell mum I'll be back soon.'

I could see my mum in the back of the bar, pouring her heart out on the phone to my auntie. Now was a good chance to slip out. There was someone I had to see.

Where I was heading wasn't far from the pub – about ten minutes' walk across the West Chalk side of Chalk Gap.

It was Carol who answered the door.

'Hello, Edward love. Now's not a good time, I'm afraid.'

I took a deep breath. My aversion to confrontation had been getting a real testing these last couple of days.

'I'm sorry, Carol, I need to speak to Brian urgently. My brother's just been arrested for the murder and I think it's because of something your husband told the police.'

Carol's jaw dropped to the floor. She knew nothing about this.

'Brian!' she shrieked at the top of her voice, making me jump. 'Edward's here for you. What have you gone and done?'

'Oh, for god's sake!' I heard from inside.

'You better come in, love,' she said as solemnly as she could manage.

Carol and Brian's front room was every middle-aged couple's front room I imagined. Floral wallpaper, leather furnishings and 'live laugh love' on the wall over the sofa. There didn't seem to have been much laughing or loving going on recently.

I glanced over at their bookcase, although there was only one shelf not given over to various ornaments and photos instead of books. I spotted a few cookbooks from TV chefs, as well as celebrity biographies of Simon Cowell, David Beckham and various other celebrities – the type of books received as Christmas presents that clog up the bestseller charts for most of winter. I saw a Stephen Hawking book which might have belonged to Brian, and a GCSE Maths text book, but otherwise the few 'literary' offers here were - like the floral room – probably all Carol. Just to confirm my thought that she was in charge of the relationship, the woman herself spoke.

'Come on then, Brian, out with it,' she said in a tone which fitted the frosty atmosphere in the room. 'Have you shopped his brother to the police?'

I thought about correcting the word 'shopped', which suggested he'd told them something Alfie actually *had* done, but I thought better of it. I remembered Carol's dislike of the police this morning.

'I can do as I please,' Brian said weakly. 'Edward thought it was me and Linda's been gossiping to the police about my drinking. Thought I'd show them the culprit might be closer to home than they thought.'

'Brian,' I started as I sat down on the sofa opposite his armchair. 'I don't mind that you did it, I just need to know. I can imagine what you said, but I want to hear about it from you.'

'Go on then, what do you think?' he eyed me suspiciously.

'You said you'd been keeping it to yourself. It was something you noticed last night in the pub, wasn't it?'

He nodded, not taking his eyes off me.

'Will one of you tell me what you're talking about?' Carol demanded.

'I don't know exactly why yet,' I started, 'but I think what Brian noticed last night is that a button was missing from Alfie's shirt. Brian, did you tell the police you think the button they found belongs to my brother?'

24

'Brian Fletcher, you are an idiot!' Carol was not happy. 'How many years have I been friends with Linda? I'll never be able to look at her again.'

'But what if he did it?' Brian offered weakly.

'What? Don't be so stupid!' She jumped up and flew over to him. I thought she would hit him. 'I'm so sorry about him, Edward. You're sorry as well, aren't you, Brian?'

Brian looked defiant before deciding on what was apparently the safest course of action. 'Yes, I am sorry. I just did what I thought was right.'

'Rubbish!' Carol started again. 'You did it because sometimes you're a petty, spiteful man. God knows what else you're capable of when the mood takes you.'

'And there we have it, Edward,' Brian remarked. I was worried about my brother and didn't want to get in the middle of this.

'She's on my case for daring to suspect your brother, and here she is suspecting her own husband! She thinks I did it.'

'I never said that, did I? And anyway you didn't just suspect him, did you? You reported him to the bloody police! Of all the things to do, honestly.'

She sat down again, and I could tell her anger had turned to upset. It had been a hard day for everyone but Carol more than most.

'Sorry about that Edward, we shouldn't be arguing in front of you. You're going through enough.' She seemed weary. 'What's the latest then? How is your mum coping?'

'She's knocked for six, to be honest,' I said. 'We don't know what's happening. I've left messages for DI Appleby but not heard yet. They can keep him for 24 hours before they charge him.'

'Oh, the poor thing,' Carol replied. 'But I don't understand, why would his button be there in the first place? If he's done nothing wrong, I mean.'

I glanced at her and she became flustered.

'Sorry, of course he's done nothing wrong. I mean, what's it all about? What was he doing there?'

I'd thought about this a lot in the last hour or so, and I had nothing. 'I've no idea. That's why I need Brian's help. Brian, I need you to tell me exactly what you saw last night.'

'Not much really, it's as I told the police.'

'Brian Fletcher, you got his brother arrested. Now so help me, God, tell him everything he wants to know right now!'

He sighed. I'd never seen the two of them together much over the years and didn't know if their behaviour was because of the stresses of the day or they were par for the course. Either way, I could see why Carol had said it wasn't a good time to call.

'Okay, so first, I wasn't as drunk as everyone thinks, I can still remember things when I'm in that pub you know.' He showed a lot of pride for someone who had been embarrassing himself regularly lately. Carol rolled her eyes and made a 'humph' noise.

'When I first got there, your mum was on the bar and your brother wasn't there. Which was different from normal, I noticed straightaway. Usually on a Friday your brother is on 'til about seven, then your mum takes over for the Friday night karaoke shift.'

He was right. Mum loved working the karaoke shifts; it was one of her stipulations when they handed the pub over to my brother. Alfie usually worked Friday afternoons and then stuck around in the evening playing pool and having some drinks, only jumping on the bar to help if it got busy. I made a mental note to check with mum about what happened yesterday.

'What time was this?'

'About five o'clock.'

'No wonder I had to drag you out of there. Starting drinking at that time…' Carol muttered.

'Anyway,' he continued, ignoring her. 'I always stand at the bar when I first get there as it's usually quiet. I asked your mum why she was on early and she said Alfie had to sort something out in Brighton but he was due back by then.'

My heart sank. This wasn't looking good so far.

'Nearly an hour later, would have been about ten to six I reckon, he came rushing in all flustered, apologising. Your mum said not to worry, but he seemed stressed. She went off to have dinner with your dad upstairs before the evening shift, Alfie came on the bar. But he was jumpy, kept checking his phone. I tried to start a conversation a couple of times, but he was having none of it. Not like him at all.'

Truthfully, it was a little like Alfie, but he's so professional that the customers would never know that. He doesn't have the problems I have, but he's always struggled with stress. The unusual part was showing it in the pub.

'Okay, so then what happened?'

'Nothing much else, he was just quiet. I didn't think much of it, just that he'd probably had an argument with his missus or something. But then I remembered he's not like that, is he?'

'Brian!' Carol scolded from her seat.

'You know what I mean. He could have a boyfriend. I wouldn't care, you know that, Carol. But he doesn't, does he?'

That last question was to me. My brother had a love life as barren as mine since the nasty breakup with his ex, Max, a year ago.

I shook my head and he continued. 'While I was sat at the bar, I noticed he had a button missing on his shirt. The one after the top one. The top one you normally have open, but that one you don't and I noticed it, I don't know why. I thought nothing of it 'til Carol told me you two saw a button near the body.'

'And then you put two and two together and made five,' Carol sniped. 'Anyway Edward, I'll walk back with you and see how your mother is. Least we can do. Give me a minute.' She gave Brian the worst look she could muster and went out of the room.

Left on our own, Brian didn't know what to say. We'd always got on well, but I knew his faults – not least his temper – especially after a drink or two.

'I'm sorry, Edward. I should have had a word with your mum and dad, not told the police. I was angry and I'd been drinking.'

Without another word, he followed Carol out of the room. I heard him go upstairs and almost immediately start arguing. I tried to ignore it. I had so much more to think about than Brian and Carol's marriage.

What was Alfie doing at school? Why did he lie to my mum about being in Brighton? And how was his button in Miss Finch's office? I had some investigating to do.

25

Carol and I turned out of the small Mews that she and Brian lived on and started the walk up West Chalk Road towards the high street. East and West Chalk Roads, along with Chalk Gap High Street and Chalk Gap Road leading to the village from the A259, were initially the only roads in our village. As demand for housing had increased in the last decade or so, they built eight sets of Mews off East Chalk and West Chalk roads.

Many residents were unhappy about these as they were building on the old farmland behind the main roads, but they were built anyway. Brian, the school union rep and the first to join any cause, was quite heavily involved in the unsuccessful protests, so it quite surprised us when he and Carol quietly moved into one of the new houses a year or so later.

As we started walking, I turned back and glanced at our old school site just behind me. Apparently the two of them had bought their current house to be closer to work, so the new site being at the far East side of the village would have been a minor inconvenience for them. Rumour has it (I'm never too far away from the latest rumours, thanks to my mum) that our old site was to be yet more new housing, this time luxury apartments. I wondered if Brian would lead the protest this time, now he was unemployed.

We walked in silence for the first couple of minutes. This was quite unlike Carol, but she was probably still upset after arguing with Brian. Either that or she had something to hide. I had now formulated a plan to get to the bottom of my brother's situation, but I also had to give as much attention to digging around the other suspects and their likelihood of doing it. Carol suspected her husband, and I had a chance to find out why.

'Don't worry about what Brian told the police,' I said to break the silence. I'd decided Alfie was a good way to get her talking about her husband indirectly. 'I'm sure he'll be alright.'

'I could kill him for doing that to your family,' she said, then paused and realised what she'd said. 'Just an expression.'

'Don't worry,' I attempted a laugh. 'We're all so paranoid about everything we say and do now, it's natural. We're all suspecting our loved ones even. We don't know who to trust.'

'Yes, I suppose.' I could feel her eyeing me suspiciously as we walked.

I decided to go for it. This was an enormous lie, but I had to say it as convincingly as I could. 'The thing is, and please don't tell my mum, I've even started to think my brother might have done it.'

She looked at me again. 'Don't say that, love.'

'It's true, I have. What do you think? Is it alright to suspect someone in your close family like that?'

There was silence for a moment; she was thinking how to reply. 'It's okay, love. Don't feel guilty. Like Brian said, I even accused him earlier. My own husband and I asked him if he did it.'

I had her. 'But why? What made you think that?'

She clammed up again. 'I don't know, I just did. It was only because of how drunk and angry he was last night.'

'How were things when you got home from the pub?'

'What you'd expect after that scene he made. We argued for a bit, I stormed off to bed and he stayed on the couch.' Carol focused on the street ahead. Being able to answer without looking at me seemed to encourage her to be more open.

'Did he fall asleep straight away? Did you hear him at all?'

'Edward love, don't do your detective stuff on me.'

'Sorry. I was just trying to get a picture of what happened. Brian asked me to prove he was innocent, so I'm making a start by asking you about last night.'

She stopped and looked at me for the first time in a few minutes. 'I think you need to focus on your brother first, love.'

'I am, but I need to work out who did it so I've got something to go to the police with.'

'It wasn't my Brian,' she blurted, defensively.

'I mean the more innocent people like Brian we can eliminate the better, so we can find out who's guilty.'

'He's not even an official suspect.'

But you are, I thought to myself.

Seemingly predicting my mental slight on her, she added, 'Seems like your brother is the only official suspect at the moment.'

At that moment, we turned on to Chalk Gap Road, which merges into the high street. I say 'high street', it's about as 'high' as a village street gets, with no more than fifteen small shops and businesses. The North end of the high street houses the more functional things like our doctor, dentist, vet and hairdressers. It was as we passed these places I realised time was running out for me to get to the bottom of this issue with Carol and

Brian.

'Carol, I've known you a long time and I respect you. I'm just going to ask you straight. I think I know why you suspect Brian.'

'Go on.' I could feel her looking at me, but I carried on looking forward.

'You think he stole your keys, don't you?'

This was met with silence. I looked over at her as we walked. She met my eyes and didn't speak, but slowly nodded her head.

'And put them back the next morning before you went to work?'

Silence again. Not even a nod this time.

'But it doesn't make sense,' I continued. 'The CCTV was taken but the swipe records were still there. You tried to access it for me in your office, but the police got there first. If Brian had taken yours, it would have shown up as you - DI Appleby would have had you in for it.'

'I told you love, that DI has not got a clue what he's doing.'

'He's following some wrong leads, but he's smart, I think. Besides, he told me he knew which ID had entered the building.'

'Did he?' She said sharply.

'Well, he told me it was none of my business.'

She paused again, obviously in thought. 'I suppose I might as well tell you, there was an ID I forgot to mention when we checked this morning. There was a spare skeleton set of keys and ID not assigned to anyone. Whoever it was probably got hold of that somehow, so that jumped up policeman will be none the wiser who used it.'

'Where was this spare ID kept, in your office?'

'I'm not sure where,' she replied quickly and curtly in a manner that said, *don't ask further*. Why was she so worried it was Brian? It was just as likely someone in school yesterday who stole the spare set while they were in.

By now we were coming to Chalk Gap Square, which hosted my family's pub. Carol was keen to change the subject, and we talked for the last couple of minutes about my brother and how my mum would be coping.

As we arrived, the pub had the closed sign on, so I knocked. My family lived upstairs, but I'd politely returned my keys when I moved in with Patrick and Kat. I'm kept awake enough without worrying I'm going to get mugged in the night for my pub keys.

My dad came and let us in, and the scene that followed was pretty much as I expected. Carol ran over to my mum, then there were lots of hugs and tears while Mum dragged her over to a table to repeat the story for probably the tenth time that day. I wondered if Carol would tell her it was Brian who went to the police. Luckily for her, mum didn't seem to have figured that out yet.

One thing I didn't expect was to find Patrick sat at one of the other tables having a pint with my dad.

'I came from the police station,' he explained. 'I spoke to DI Appleby and he accepted my story. I think I'm in the clear for now.'

'One down, one to go,' my dad said. 'Just your brother to go now.'

'I won't hold my breath,' Mum said from her table, interrupting her own story to Carol. 'No offence to you, Patrick love, but I don't see why that Inspector has got time to see you straight away but not return my calls.'

Poor mum. The police had wanted to speak to Patrick urgently to establish his whereabouts over the last 24 hours. It was natural that Appleby would prioritise that over returning the calls of another suspect's pestering mother.

'And don't even get me started on them turning up with a warrant in the first place, she continued. 'I'm sure you can't do that with no reason to, and you can't arrest someone with no evidence. He's only done it because it's your brother.'

Mum made a good point. She didn't know about

the button, but a tip-off from Brian shouldn't have led immediately to a search warrant. And even once they confirmed the button was Alfie's, it only proved that he'd been in school – not that he was the murderer. Whether it was poor police work or deliberate targeting, it didn't seem right.

But I didn't have long to ponder this. No one had locked the door again when we came in, so it surprised me when Appleby himself appeared. Everyone in the room fell to a sudden hush and stared at the new arrival.

'What are you doing here, DI Appleby?' I used his police name intentionally to get my parents up to speed on who he was.

It worked. 'Is this him?' My mum jumped straight to her feet and leapt in front of him. 'Speak of the devil and he shall appear!'

My mum isn't religious at all, but she likes her clichés.

'Well, well, well, looks like the gang's all here!' Appleby said with a cliché of his own as he noticed Carol and Patrick. 'What's this, a suspect get together?'

'Don't you come here getting smart!' my mum said while Dad sat quietly with Patrick. For all of my dad's jovial loudness, he hated confrontation. Unluckily for him he married my mum.

'I don't want an argument, Mrs Crisp,' Appleby

said.

'Worked out who I am, have you? That's probably the best detective work you've done all day.'

'I shouldn't even be here,' Appleby replied, ignoring the insult.

'Oh, shouldn't you now?' my mum said. 'We can soon get your Chief Inspector on the phone about you harassing victim's families.'

I didn't tell her that the DCI was a close friend of 'that flash b word' Tim.

'Actually, Mrs Crisp, you'll find I'm allowed to visit suspects and gather information from their families. But I came to help you out. I'm sorry, my colleagues passed on all of your messages. I've had a very busy evening.' He glanced over slyly at Patrick. 'But I thought I'd make up for it by coming round in person.'

Mum seemed suspicious about his sudden niceness. 'How can you help us then? When are you letting my son out?'

'Never, if you don't let me explain why I'm here.' He looked at me. 'Edward, am I okay to speak in front of everyone?'

'Course you are,' Mum snapped. 'They're our friends and we've got nothing to hide.'

'I just wanted to check, because technically

they're also suspects in the case.'

Carol looked outraged.

'I will speak off the record, honestly,' he continued. 'I'm not sure that Alfie murdered Miss Finch.'

'Oh well done, Sherlock!' Mum shouted.

'Of course he didn't!' My dad finally broke his silence. 'Why aren't you releasing him then?'

'It's not as simple as that. As I'm sure you know, we have 24 hours to investigate a suspect without charging them. We're only a few hours into that.'

As usual, my mind was working overtime, and I saw where this was going. 'Alfie isn't co-operating with you, is he? You can't find any motive for him, but he won't tell you why he was at the school.'

'Edward, what are you saying?' Mum said. 'He wasn't at the school, he was in Brighton.'

'I'm afraid I can't disclose details, but we have evidence that suggests Alfie was at school at some point between Friday afternoon and Miss Finch's murder.'

Mum still had no clue about the button. Carol looked sheepish, no doubt hoping that he wouldn't mention how they knew about the button.

'So you need Alfie to tell you the truth about why he was there, even if it's nothing to do with the murder.'

'Exactly right, thank you, Edward.' I noticed that Appleby had been a picture of politeness to me so far. 'Can any of you think of anything that would help that he hasn't told us?'

'Don't be stupid, he was probably just looking for his brother for something,' my mum said.

'I doubt he'd find Edward on the floor of Miss Finch's office,' Appleby replied with a smirk which immediately dropped when he realised he'd said too much. This was enough for mum.

'Now, listen you. Don't get smart with us, coming round here with lies about Alfie. You've made one of my son's lives a misery, you're not going to do it to my other one. That's right, I know exactly who you are. My Edward might be frightened of you, but I'm not.'

Thanks mum, I thought, though otherwise I was quite enjoying this. Appleby had come round to help and my mum had got the wrong idea because she didn't know about the button. Still, a petty side of me enjoyed seeing Appleby suffer for once.

'Just tell your son to stop lying to the police.' He looked at me. 'In fact, tell both your sons.'

I noticed that Appleby didn't take criticism well, and this usually caused his retreat into this smug persona. Having apparently decided he'd had the last word, he turned to walk back out.

'Excuse me Inspector, you forgot something,'

my mum said ever so politely.

And when he turned round, she slapped him straight in the face.

26

I was expecting all chaos to break loose.

Appleby slowly rubbed his face. ‘Edward, can I speak to you outside, mate?’

My mum flew forward again. ‘So you can threaten him without us hearing? I don’t think so. You can arrest me for assault first.’

‘No, he cannot,’ my dad said, stepping forward to join her.

‘I’m not going to arrest anyone else.’ His inclusion of this last word was a reminder he was in control. He looked me straight in the eye. ‘Edward... please, mate?’

He was offering us an olive branch. Mum was being protective, I understood that, but I had to stand on my own. ‘Mum, I think he’s trying to help us. I’m going to speak to him.’

Not wanting a second family member arrested in the same day, my dad convinced her, but the compromise was that Patrick would come with us.

The three of us sat on the bench across the village square. Patrick was awkwardly in between us, next to the police detective who had considered him a potential murderer just hours ago.

It was Appleby who spoke first. 'I'm gonna allow your mum that, mate.'

'You are?' I asked.

'I'm not the slimeball you all think I am, you know.'

Honestly, I couldn't decide about Appleby. He still seemed capable of slipping into his arrogant, bullying persona, and this time he had been embarrassed at the hands of a middle-aged woman. But was this a peace-making gesture or his way of preventing an embarrassing story from getting out?

'Thanks, I appreciate it.' Either way, he was trying, and it paid to stay on the right side of the SIO of the investigation. It's a shame my mum didn't think so.

'Just do one thing for me. Find out what your brother's hiding from us.'

'I thought you told me not to investigate?'

'Just this one thing. You're in a good position to do it.' He rubbed his sore cheek a little. 'That's the only thing you're to do, do you hear me, mate? I'm the detective here.' His arrogant persona was back.

'Tell your mum there's no hard feelings.' He shook my hand and turned to shake Patrick's, addressing him next. 'And no more disappearing acts from you, please. Stay out of trouble, both of you.'

He stood up and walked across the square to where his car was parked. 'Oh, and Edward? Don't worry, mate, I will catch whoever did this.' We watched him get in his car and drive off before I spoke again.

'Not if I do first.'

'Complicated history between you two, isn't it?' Patrick said. 'He seems like he's on your side though.'

'Yeah, I guess.'

'You don't think your brother did it, do you?'

'I know he didn't. But I also know he's lying about something.' I decided to go for it and find out what Patrick was still hiding. 'Like I know you are too.'

'What do you mean?'

'Your story earlier. There's something missing.'

'What's missing then?' I could hear the dubious tone in his voice when he answered.

'You said the meeting yesterday was the first time you'd seen Miss Finch since before the summer holidays. But in the meeting she said she'd seen you yesterday.'

'No, she didn't.'

'She did, Patrick. If I'm going to solve this, I need you to be honest.'

'Edward, will you listen to yourself? You're getting carried away. Appleby's right. He's the detective, not you. Do what you can to get Alfie out of jail, but leave me out of it. I'm done with it. See you later.'

He walked across the square and back towards the high street. I'd have to find out what he was hiding later. It was time to get my brother out of jail.

27

'I'm sorry Ed, I can't think of any legitimate reasons your brother would have been in her office.'

Kat and I sat at our kitchen table as I told her everything that had happened. There was no sign of Patrick at home and his car wasn't outside - he was probably still sulking with me. I used the time on my own with Kat to pick her brains; she was in the office next door to Finch. I admired how straight up Kat always was, but this wasn't what I wanted to hear.

'Are they sure it was definitely his button?' she asked. 'How would he even have got access to the school?'

I told her the story of Brian and the button, that the police came with a warrant, took lots of his clothes, the button was definitely his but he was offering them no explanation for his presence at the school. I saw Kat's face change, and I thought she was probably starting to think he did it.

But I knew it wasn't him, and I thought I knew

why he was in Miss Finch's office; even without information from Kat, I trusted my hunch. I took my phone from my pocket and sent a message before moving her on to talk about the other suspects.

'Out of all our colleagues on the access list, who do you think could have done it?'

'I don't know,' she replied. 'It's insane to think we're working with a murderer, but it's looking like we are. Maybe Tim, I suppose? He's the nastiest piece of work out of everyone on that list. And I feel awful saying it, but I just can't see it being any of the others.'

'Not even Brian using Carol's keys?'

'No Ed, Brian's just an old windbag. He's all mouth, but he'd never do something like this. He's a good guy overall when he's not moaning about everything.'

'So you don't think Tim's a good guy?'

'There's something about him, Ed. I can't put my finger on it, but I just don't trust him. I've worked with him for two years since he's been governor and I just can't warm to him. You saw the way he spoke to Finch when you were here that day.'

That reminded me of something else I had to ask her. 'What did you mean when you said to me "watch this space" that day? What did you know?'

'I knew you would ask me that,' she smiled.

'Attention to detail. You're wasted as a school librarian.'

I felt myself blush at the compliment. It embarrassed me that people thought of me as 'just' the school librarian sometimes. I knew my anxiety had held me back from my other plans.

'I see and hear a lot working up there,' she said, returning to the question I asked her. 'With Tim you never know what side he's on. We were all in school together a lot over summer and, as you saw the other day, things weren't as rosy as people think between those two.'

I tried to recall what I'd heard about them when Miss Finch first arrived. 'Didn't he know her before she got the job?'

'I heard that too, but they were always sketchy about it, even in front of me. I know that Tim is the link to the academy chain; he knew someone there and persuaded the rest of the board they were the right people for us.'

'And she came from the academy, didn't she?' I remembered out loud.

'Yeah and they were always on the same side from the outset. At my expense, usually. It should be the Head and Deputy running the school together. The Chair of Governors shouldn't be so hands on. But he was always there, thick as thieves with her. Until recently, anyway.'

'What happened?'

'This is where it gets interesting. In the last couple of weeks there was definitely some kind of falling out between Finch and Tim.'

I noticed Kat's enjoyment of these words as she spoke them. I had to remember this wasn't an unbiased account. She'd wanted to be Head Teacher desperately before they appointed Miss Finch, and since then had been left out so much by the two of them she barely seemed like the Deputy Head anymore.

'But you've no idea what about?'

'I'm not sure,' she said. 'But I have seen a couple of frosty exchanges over the last couple of weeks. The interesting part though is that they were both trying to get rid of one another.'

'What?' This was a revelation.

'Tim talks so loudly on the phone you can hear him through the glass walls. I came in early one morning and he didn't know I was there. I realised he was talking to someone from the academy board and I heard him mention another academy Head Teacher and whether they would be available to come and replace Miss Finch in the next few weeks.'

I wasn't expecting that. 'You're joking. When was this?'

‘About two weeks ago.’ This put Tim further into the frame. Why was he expecting Miss Finch to need replacing for around the time she was murdered?

‘That’s not all,’ she continued. ‘I told Dylan about it to see if he knew any more, and he told me he was delivering post to Miss Finch and had overheard a similar conversation. But in this one, she was talking to another governor about holding a vote of no confidence in Tim as Chair.’

‘Wow, so it was mutual backstabbing? Who was first?’

‘We compared notes and Dylan said he’d overheard Finch the day before, so she was. One of the other governors must have warned Tim, and then he tried to strike back by going to the academy.’

This opened up all kinds of possibilities. Was Tim trying to save his own position? Did his plan to get Miss Finch out fail so he had to resort to murder? And what caused their argument?

As much as my heart was telling me otherwise, I couldn’t forget Kat. I had to be impartial and look at every suspect.

‘Do you think they’ll still bring in this temporary Head from the academy then, or is there a chance they could give it to you for the time being?’

'Funnily enough, Tim called me about that this morning. A couple of weeks ago they could have put someone in, but everyone is already assigned to their school for September now and they don't have anyone immediately available. He said they will have an emergency governors' meeting next week, but he's proposing to put me in as Acting Head.'

So Kat benefitted from this situation. I didn't ask her any more questions about herself as I didn't want her to think I was even considering her. But either way, I was saved from this by the doorbell ringing.

'Oh hi, Dylan!' I heard her say brightly from the hallway. 'I wasn't expecting you, have you heard anything more about the murder?'

I heard him say he was here to see me, before he shuffled into the kitchen looking confused – his usual confident smile missing. He looked worried about something. And I knew what that something was.

'Kat, are you okay to give me and Dylan five minutes?'

'I have stuff to do anyway – someone's got to keep this house clean haven't they, Ed? See you boys in a while.' She smiled and left the room; she probably just thought I would ask Dylan the same things I'd asked her.

'Dylan, there's someone important you've not heard from this evening, isn't there? And you're wondering why.'

'I don't know what you're talking about -' he started, but I cut him off.

'Dylan, I'm going to come straight to the point. Earlier today, the police arrested my brother because they found his shirt button near Miss Finch's body. You need to tell the police you're in a relationship with Alfie.'

28

I'd worked it out after a lot of thinking. There was no way that my brother had killed Miss Finch. And yet the button was his.

I'd racked my brains. Alfie had no connection to Miss Finch that I knew of, nor could I think of one. It occurred to me that if Alfie wasn't gay, an explanation could have been something going on between him and Kat I didn't know about.

But then I realised – there wasn't just Kat in those offices, there was Dylan too. Young, handsome, easy to like Dylan – who had mentioned little about his private life or a girlfriend. A connection between the two of them was the only reason I could think of for Alfie being in the school leadership suite. But if that was true, why didn't Alfie just tell the police?

Then I remembered Dylan's phone conversation and the subsequent chat we had. Some of it had been fabrication for the benefit of the old lady, but I remembered two parts that were true. Dylan had recently moved to the village with his widowed mother, and they were a strict catholic family. What if he was in the closet and couldn't come out for fear of what his mum would think? That would explain why Alfie refused to speak – he was trying to protect him.

It turned out I was right - even though he hadn't spoken yet. I could tell by Dylan's tears. As you can probably guess by now, this made me uncomfortable, but I just kept awkwardly repeating that it was okay until he was ready to speak.

When he eventually did, he said just one thing. 'Edward, let's go and get him.'

We stayed in silence for the first few minutes of the car journey as Dylan drove us to Lewes police station. Eventually, he told me his story.

'We met on a dating app when I first moved to the village a few months ago. I didn't even use a photo, so it surprised me when someone wanted to talk to me.'

'Then what?' Sharing private lives wasn't something my brother and I did (not that I have one to share), but I needed to hear this story. This was the story that would get Alfie out of jail.

'We met up a couple of times and liked each other, and before we knew it we were seeing each other. But I asked him to keep it quiet because of mum. So we met in secret – going for drives, meeting far away.' He focused perfectly on the road ahead as he continued. 'Then over summer we started to meet at school a little, once Kat and Miss Finch had left for the day.'

'So that's what happened yesterday before the murder?'

'Yes!' he blurted out, sounding annoyed with himself. 'Edward, I could kick myself! We usually go into one of the empty offices, my desk is too visible right in the open. But I can't believe he's let them keep him in for nothing. It's all my fault!'

It happened exactly as I'd thought. But this wasn't Dylan's fault – he hadn't even known about the arrest. 'Don't worry, we can get him out now. And look at it this way – Alfie must really like you to not tell them. It's all going to be fine now.'

That's what I told him in the car. As for now, I was sat in Lewes police station waiting while he was in with Appleby telling the whole story.

But that meant the killer was still out there. I still couldn't eliminate Dylan completely, though I couldn't see it being my brother's new boyfriend, and even Patrick was still lying to me about something. It worried me that Appleby would turn his attention to Noah now that he had no evidence against Patrick and my brother.

Appleby came out to the reception area with Alfie. He headed over to speak to me as my brother was being signed out by the desk sergeant, with Dylan heading straight over to him.

'I knew you'd sort it out, mate,' the D.I. said. 'You did well, cheers.'

'Thank you,' I replied. 'I was worried you were just going to charge him.'

'I believe in the truth mate, and I knew that wasn't the truth. It's got nothing to do with it being your brother, just knew he was innocent.'

Appleby wouldn't admit it, but it felt like we were on the same side.

'That means the real culprit is still out there,' I said.

'Don't go getting any ideas, mate. I meant what I said, leave it to us now.' Then he stopped for a minute and thought. 'What do you make of that caretaker? Do you think she's got something to hide?'

I really couldn't work him out. One moment he was telling me not to get involved and the next he was asking my opinion on suspects.

'I'm not sure,' I said, not wanting to commit myself. 'I really can't see it.' But I thought this about almost everyone, and it had to be one of them.

'It was her husband who told us about your brother, you know. But she was there last night comforting your mum. What are those two up to?'

His implication was accurate; Carol and Brian had been involved in the case at every turn. It was just then that I remembered something Appleby might help me with.

'You said you wouldn't tell me about the swipe card records but if I made an educated guess and you confirmed it, that wouldn't be the same thing, would it?'

'Shush!' he said, glancing over to the desk sergeant. 'Come out here.' He gestured outside, and I followed him through the front entrance.

'Go on,' he said dubiously.

'It wasn't one person's ID that accessed the leadership suite, it was the spare.'

'How do you know – I mean, what makes you think that?' He caught himself too late not to give it away. I could see him thinking. 'Carol Fletcher told you, didn't she? I think I need to look into her more closely.'

For the record, I'd believed everything Carol had told me and didn't want to make him suspect her. 'I told you, I don't think it's her. She even had a big argument with Brian because she suspected him.'

'Her own husband... Miss Finch fired him, didn't she? The Governor bloke told us about that. And then Brian Fletcher tried to put us on to your brother. He's always been rotten, even when I was at school.' He was one to talk. 'Yes mate, I think I know where to look next.'

After what Kat had told me, 'the governor bloke' maybe wasn't so innocent himself. But there was definitely more to the story with Carol and Brian, so it wouldn't do any harm to let Appleby pursue them next while I focused on Tim, who I was yet to even question.

'I'm still keeping my eye on your young helper too, mate,' he warned. 'I know you think there's no chance, but you'll learn anything's possible in a murder case.' I wasn't overly impressed by his patronising tone.

'Jamie, there's no way Noah had anything to do with it. He might be obsessed with murders, but he'd have no idea how to carry one out.'

As he was about to argue back, Alfie and Dylan joined us outside.

'Thank you so much, bro,' my brother said as he came and hugged me. 'I should have told the truth, but I was worried about Dylan.' He smiled at his boyfriend. 'But we'll get through it together.'

'Just make sure you tell the truth if we ever have reason to talk to you again,' Appleby warned him.

While my brother's part in the case was hopefully over, mine wasn't. I'd been putting it off but I couldn't any longer. It was time to question our Chair of Governors.

29

As I got out of the car and walked across the gravel driveway to Tim's beautiful converted farmhouse, I realised this was probably one of the nicest residences in Chalk Gap.

Dylan had dropped me off, and now he and Alfie would have to brave Mum. I'd promised that I would call in later to see them. I thought Mum's usual Sunday afternoon lunch would have been off today, but the moment she knew that Alfie was free I was sure she would drive into Eastbourne to get everything she needed.

I'd decided to just turn up on Tim's doorstep, under the pretence of coming to tell him about my brother being released. Obviously we weren't on those kinds of terms – I'd never been to his house before – but Tim was self-important enough to not think twice about someone coming in person to give him an update.

I was sat awkwardly waiting for him to finish a phone call in their spacious open plan living room. Lots of space, but not much in it; I saw a dresser with a few photos on it, but I noted there was no bookcase or bookshelves, and therefore no books in sight. Gracie was technically reading as she waited with me - perched on a chair arm, scrolling through one of her social media feeds on her phone and looking bored.

'It's a bit creepy, isn't it?' She mused. 'A member of staff visiting a student at home.'

'I'm just here to see your dad, Gracie.'

'Daddy's on the phone to the Chief Inspector. They're good friends, you know. He's trying to find out if they've charged your brother or not,' she said with a cruel smile on her face.

'Actually, they haven't, they made a mistake,' I blurted. I was disappointed with myself for getting drawn into her games. 'That's what I came round to tell your dad.'

'So it's one of the other suspects,' she said. 'I enjoy being a suspect. They don't think I did it, though. I don't know why.'

'You're not a member of staff and they know it's unlikely you've done it. They'll want to look at more obvious suspects first.' And because 'Daddy' had a word with his friend the DCI, I thought.

'What about Noah? I bet he's high on their list.' She smirked as she said this.

'Why are you so mean to Noah?'

She seemed surprised by this but, before she

could answer, I continued.

'I'm going to tell you something about the detective who questioned us all.'

'What about him?' She looked mildly interested.

'We went to school together, and he used to bully me.' The pain of the memories came back. 'Relentlessly bully me. It's stuck with me my whole life.'

She looked at me. The smirk had gone, and she looked a little shaken.

'I hadn't seen him for 15 years until the interview yesterday. I was terrified at first, seeing him after all this time and him having power over me again. But what I'm telling you isn't about me. It's about DI Appleby. The first thing he did was apologise to me for everything. I could tell it had stayed with him all these years.'

I didn't add that he technically never said the words 'I'm sorry' but I was allowing it so I could make my point. She sat silently for a moment, not looking at me. When she spoke, her eyes scanned her childhood photos on the dresser. 'I'm not a bully. I hate that word. I only mean it as a joke.'

'It's not a joke though. I know Noah seems oblivious to it, but words hurt. And you should grow up being proud of your actions, not ashamed of them like Jamie Appleby.'

There was another long silence. I could hear

Tim's sycophantic tone as he talked to the DCI on the phone in the next room.

'I'm not a horrible person. I know you think I am, and I don't care.' She wasn't exactly helping her point. 'It just annoys me when Noah starts being weird.'

'He has Asperger's.'

'I know.' Her voice had fallen quiet, but suddenly she turned to look at me and her gaze was like a pickaxe. 'I'll leave off him, but not because you told me.' She paused again before continuing, much less confidently, in a murmur. 'You think you know the whole story, but you don't.'

'What are you talking about?'

She rolled her eyes. 'I'm not going to tell you, obviously.' She focused on the photos again.

'Something about you, or Noah?' Her sudden change had surprised me, and I couldn't think what she meant.

'I said I'm not going to tell you. I can't. But you wouldn't think I was horrible if you knew.' Her voice was softer now, almost gentle. She stood up and started walking out. 'I'm off out riding now. I'll tell my dad to hurry up on my way out.'

Another secret. Something that would make me think Gracie wasn't such a horrible person. For the record, I didn't think that, anyway. I just thought she was an immature, spoiled girl with a nasty tongue.

But this felt like a big clue. From the way she looked at those old photos as she spoke, I was sure she meant something to do with her upbringing.

'Ah Edward, I've just heard from the DCI about your brother!' Tim walked in as confidently as I'd expect him to in his own home. 'Gracie said you came round to tell me. That's kind of you. Such tough times for us all, we have to stick together.'

His words were nice, although they felt like insincere, empty platitudes. I had to make the most of my opportunity to speak to him alone; it might have been my only one. So I had to play the game.

'Thank you Tim, I hope you don't mind me coming to see you.'

'Not at all. I was going to touch base with all the staff, anyway. Particularly you after this business with your brother. I'm glad it's sorted out. Though I'm not happy with Dylan carrying on his liaisons on school premises, I'll be having a word with him.'

He suddenly looked embarrassed. 'Nothing to do with anything like that.' I assumed 'anything like that,' meant being gay. 'I'd say the same if he'd sneaked a young lady in.'

'Did the DCI mention that Dylan wants to keep this quiet?'

'Of course, no issue there. None of my business

once I've had a word. He's an exemplary employee, ever since he joined the academy.'

This was a good opportunity to start my questioning. 'Oh yes, he worked with Miss Finch at her last school, didn't he? She must have valued Dylan to bring him with her.'

I saw his face change at the mention of Miss Finch by name. He almost looked upset, which was the first genuine emotion I'd seen from him. Despite their recent betrayals of one another, they must have been close before that; Miss Finch had come to us on Tim's recommendation.

'Sorry, Edward,' he said as he composed himself. 'I still can't get used to Anne not being here. It's horrible to think someone could do that to her. But I know the police are working hard to catch whoever is responsible.' His less sincere, public tone of voice was back.

'But Miss Finch,' I couldn't call her Anne, 'knew Dylan beforehand?' I clarified.

'Oh yes, she thought a lot of him. Why do you ask? Surely you don't suspect your brother's new partner?'

'I'm just trying to build a picture of her in my head. I didn't know her very well, I thought it would help to learn more about her.'

'Help what?' he asked. 'Why do you need to know about her?'

'DI Appleby is my old school friend. Obviously he is doing well on the case, but he asked my opinion - as someone he trusts who knows the suspects.'

Tim seemed to accept this explanation. 'Ah yes, the DCI said that DI Appleby is an excellent detective. Sensible plan, that.' Luckily, Tim wouldn't even think to include himself when I said 'suspects'.

'I just don't know too much about Miss Finch herself, that's all,' I said, building to my question. 'But you knew her beforehand too, I heard? Weren't you old friends?'

He looked at me cautiously. 'You don't need to worry about that, I told the DI everything in my interview yesterday.' Well played, Tim. He wasn't about to tell me anything he didn't need to. He had beaten me at my own game.

'It's just he only asked me this morning,' I lied. 'So he obviously wants to know more about Miss Finch. Anything you could tell me would save him from having to interview you again.' I was playing a dangerous game using Appleby's name like that. If I wasn't careful, Tim would be on the phone to the DCI again.

He narrowed his eyes as he focused on me. 'Anne and I go back years,' he said, slowly and deliberately. 'She was a brilliant Head Teacher and a loyal hard-working woman. I can't think of any reason someone would do this to her.' He could have been making a statement at a press conference appeal.

'Oh, of course,' I said. 'And you two got on very well, so I know you'll want justice. But was she going to stay at the school much longer?'

'I beg your pardon?'

'Just something I heard.' I'd said too much. I couldn't give him the details of Kat's account.

But it was too late. 'Look here, Mr Crisp,' he said, saying my formal name in a very precise and pronounced way. 'I'm not sure what you've heard, and what your intentions are, but I strongly suggest you leave this matter to the police. DCI Reid will hear that his detectives are using amateurs to snoop around. And as Chair of Governors, I'd like to advise you that your own job could be at risk if you continue to harass your colleagues at home.'

I had blown it. Tim abruptly showed me out, again muttering about snooping and how it would cost me my job. I glanced back at the doorway as he pushed me through it.

He thought he hadn't told me anything important, but he had. His reaction told me lots. There was definitely more to the story with Tim and Miss Finch.

30

'I told you he was hiding something, didn't I?'

I was on the phone to Kat as I walked along the seafront from Tim's house to the pub. I was sure she wanted him to be the culprit. She'd led me towards him, and I knew she was at least a little biased in the matter.

'The key to it is finding out how they knew each other before she came here,' I said.

'I really don't know,' she replied. 'But before the interviews for a new Head, all he did was sing her praises. I knew she would get that job before I even met her.'

'But what went on between them to cause the fall out?' I was thinking aloud rather than asking Kat directly.

'That's where you come in, Sherlock Crisp,' she laughed. 'See what Dylan thinks. Tell him you know my part of the story and get him to tell you his again. He might have missed something.'

Just then, my mum appeared at the pub door,

frantically gesturing to me and trying to usher me inside. I said goodbye to Kat and promised to update her again later. I hoped mum would accept a fleeting visit for Sunday dinner; I was hoping to pop to the café and see Emma.

'Edward love, we've all been waiting! Come on, it's a very special day.'

'Sorry mum, work stuff. I bet you're pleased Alfie's home?'

'Oh yes, love, I am, but not just that! We've got prospective new members of the family to celebrate with. Come on, the roast is ready.'

Of course. As well as my brother's freedom, Mum would also have just found out about his new romance.

She didn't seem too bothered that Dylan hadn't immediately gone to the police. I just hoped for Dylan's sake she would be discreet. I'd have a word with her.

As I followed her into the pub, the words she just used struck me. Prospective *members,* not member. A thought occurred to me and I hoped I was wrong.

I wasn't.

'Hello, Mr Crisp! Me and my mum are joining you for Sunday dinner!'

As I walked in the pub, Noah and Emma sat at

one of the tables chatting to Dylan and Alfie. What was going on?

'Emma popped in earlier to see if there was any news on Alfie. Very kind of her, she's a lovely girl,' she said, smiling over at an embarrassed Emma. 'I knew she'd want to see you so I thought I'd invite her to join us for dinner. Alfie's brought Dylan with him, so why not?'

'And they said I could come too,' Noah said happily.

Socially, this was my worst nightmare. I couldn't even comprehend all the different elements going on. It was an impromptu celebration dinner for Alfie's release, and his 'plus one' was his formerly secret boyfriend, who was still in the closet from his strict catholic mother, and just happened to be my colleague and the PA of our recently murdered Head Teacher.

Meanwhile, my mum had invited the woman I was starting to like and was treating her like she was my girlfriend already. Oh, and she had brought her socially awkward teenage son - who was my library assistant and self-appointed Doctor Watson. Is that everything?

'Come on everyone, Dad will have dinner ready by now!' my mum shouted across the pub. We started following her across the pub towards the door to our flat. Emma was at the back of the procession and I grabbed her for a moment.

'Listen, I'm sorry about this,' I whispered.

'Don't be silly, it was really kind of your mum to include us,' she replied. 'And Noah's really excited. We don't have much family to speak of, so it's nice for him. It will be fun!'

'Are you joking? Emma, it will be hell up there!'

'Edward, relax. I'm looking forward to spending time with your family.' She looked at me in a strange way I hadn't seen before. 'I don't know if you noticed but I like you, you know.' And then she leaned forward and kissed me.

31

To my surprise, the dinner itself passed without incident. Dad had made a delicious roast (as he did every week), and mum's elation over the apparent romantic fortunes of her sons, combined with Noah's happy, excitable conversation, were enough to combat any awkwardness that the rest of us might have felt at being thrown together like this.

Noah had asked my brother what it was like in a prison cell and had listened in fascination to the answer. He even stopped eating dinner to make notes on his phone. This could have been an awkward moment, but Emma had made a joke of it; she had a way of making Noah's quirks seem normal.

It was my mum's turn to put her foot in it next, grilling Dylan about being in the closet and what it was like. Dylan had seemed a little uncomfortable until Emma started talking about all the celebrities who had been in the closet, even starting a debate about some who still are, which fully interested my mum and took her away from interrogating Dylan.

As dinner finished, and we all sat with that full, lethargic feeling we always get after my dad's roasts, talk turned to the murder.

'It's got to be that flash b word in the Mercedes,' Mum said. 'I won't swear in front of our guests, but you know what I mean.' Yes mum, we always know what you mean.

'Who else could it be?' Alfie asked.

'You don't think his daughter was involved, do you?' Dylan asked. 'She's horrible when she's in our office waiting for her dad. Acts like she owns the place.'

'I know her,' my mum chipped in. 'She swans round the whole village like that.'

'You should see her when she goes out on that pony,' my dad said. 'Expects every car to crawl along two miles an hour behind her.'

'My colleague Kat says she's a bit of a bully,' Dylan added.

'She's not very nice to Noah,' Emma said, surprising me a little by joining in.

'If it's not the father, it's definitely the daughter,' my mum said.

'Or they could both be in on it!' Dad said.

'Oh, come on, it's not going to be a sixteen-year-old girl!' Alfie blurted out.

'One murderer in Agatha Christie is twelve,' Noah said. I'd heard this from him multiple times, but the others hadn't. 'She does it because her grandad won't buy her ballet shoes.'

'Bless him, he reminds me so much of my Edward,' Mum said to Emma.

'Oh, when he was that age?' Emma asked.

'Oh no, she means last week,' Dad said, jumping in with one of his unfunny jokes.

'Dylan.' I was desperate to get away from this conversation. 'I know you've had a crazy day, but I wanted to ask you a few things about Tim when we get a chance to speak.'

'You're speaking now! Just ask him now, we don't mind!'

'Mum, I don't think it would be appropriate in front of everyone – '

'Rubbish!' she replied. 'We all know the flash b word is the number 1 suspect anyway so there's no harm! And everyone here is practically family anyway.'

'Yes, I'd love to see my son in action doing his detective thing,' Dad said.

'And me!' Noah added. 'We're investigating

together, so I need to hear what Dylan says about Mr Hunt too.'

I sighed, looking at Dylan to bail me out.

'You don't have to talk about this in front of everyone,' my brother said, the only one on my side.

'It's fine, I honestly don't mind,' Dylan replied. 'The quicker I help you, the quicker you can find the culprit.'

'Well put!' Mum said, sealing the deal.

'Fine.' I gave in. 'But what we discuss stays around this table. It's confidential.'

'I don't know why you look at me when you say that!' my mum protested.

I updated Dylan (and everyone else) about everything I knew so far regarding Tim – the secret Gracie referred to, the argument I saw the day before the murder, Kat's story about Miss Finch trying to get rid of Tim and him following suit and finally how angry he got when he realised I was asking about their relationship.

'He definitely did it,' my mum said when I'd finished.

'We don't know that for sure, Mum. That's why I want to see what Dylan knows.'

Dylan confirmed his part of the story exactly as Kat had told it; Miss Finch was trying to get the other governors to hold a vote of no confidence in Tim.

'It's hardly a motive for murder though,' Alfie said. 'Governors aren't even paid positions, are they?'

'You know him, he's all about status,' Mum replied. I was sure she'd never had a conversation with Tim Hunt in her life.

'No, Alfie's right, there must be more to it than that,' I said.

'There's always a big secret we're not meant to know about,' Noah added, joining in. It was amusing to see the confusion on everyone's faces; no one except me and Emma were used to Noah's use of mystery tropes in any conversation.

'He means in murder mysteries,' Emma said, smiling.

'Yes, especially when it's the person we only suspect near the end. He'll have a secret link to the victim we didn't know about,' he said, proud to be imparting his knowledge.

'Well, I've always suspected him,' Mum said, shocking absolutely no one. 'But I think you're onto something with this secret link business.' I must admit that I'd been thinking the same thing myself.

'What do you think, Dylan?'

'There's definitely something strange,' he said. 'Until that day I heard her on the phone, they were close. They must have had a falling out.'

'Must be something serious,' Dad said. 'You don't get someone close to you sacked for just a little argument.'

'You don't know Miss Finch,' Dylan replied. 'But you have a point, they were super close. Even when I worked for her at our last school, I heard her mention Tim quite a bit and take phone calls from him. And she seemed determined to have the Head job here as soon as she heard of it. It was all "Tim's school" this and "Tim's school" that.'

'I'll tell you what I think,' my mum said, before pausing for dramatic effect. 'They're at it!' She mouthed the last two words as if they were too scandalous to say out loud.

'It makes perfect sense!' She could barely get her words out through excitement. 'They were involved with each other, he gets her the job at school so they can be together every day, but then they have a falling out and she tries to get rid of him.'

'So he gets rid of her… for good,' Dad piped up.

'And that explains his daughter's secret she wouldn't tell you… that the Head Teacher was practically her step mum.'

I didn't tell them all that this was a theory I'd

had since yesterday. But it was something Dylan said a few moments before that had stuck in my mind.

'We've been looking at this all wrong,' I said. 'Dylan, you said earlier "you don't know Miss Finch" and you're right, we don't. We know nothing about her. But we need to. I've been focusing everything on murder suspects, but I know hardly anything about the murder victim herself.'

'That's right,' Noah said. 'In murder mysteries you have to know all about the murder victim as a person to work out who killed them. It all centres around them.'

Everyone at the table looked at Dylan expectantly. He was our resident expert on Miss Finch.

'Don't look at Dylan!' my brother said.

'She was his boss,' my dad said.

'It's fine, I do know more than anyone else,' Dylan assured him. 'I just don't know how much help I can be.'

'What was she like?' I prompted. 'Was she as rude as she came across?'

'She always said she was very direct rather than rude,' Dylan replied. 'But I think she knew her position of power gave her leeway in how she could treat people and I think she enjoyed it. I overheard conversations with both Brian and Patrick where she was just nasty.' I made a mental note of this; I would come back to it later.

'But what about as a person in private? What was she like with you? Did she talk about her personal life?'

'I don't know. Nicer than she was to everyone else, I suppose.'

'That won't get us anywhere,' my mum said. 'No one will know much about her if Dylan doesn't. Just concentrate on the flash b word instead.'

'Mrs Crisp, you've given me an idea!' Dylan said suddenly.

'Oh love, call me Linda.'

'Do you fancy a trip?' He directed his words at me, not acknowledging my mum. Hopefully ignoring her was a faux pas she'd forgive him for.

'What are you talking about?' my brother asked him.

'What your mum said, it really was brilliant.'

Mum blushed – yes, he'd be fine.

'She said no one will know more than me about her, but there is someone. A couple of weeks ago I had to drop some paperwork off for Miss Finch at home. The old lady next door pretended to come out to her bin to have a nosy who I was. We were chatting away at the gate til Miss Finch came out and stopped us. I'd bet anything she knows plenty about her.'

This was a brilliant plan. I'd already seen Dylan in action with old ladies and I knew he'd be great at this. 'Let's go then.'

'You don't mind, do you?' he asked my brother.

'Of course not,' Alfie said, squeezing his hand. 'You'll be brilliant.'

'I want to come too!' Noah said at once. 'I'm your Hastings, not Dylan. No offence, Dylan.'

I could see Emma looking at me before she gave approval. What could I do? I nodded at her.

'Off you go then,' she said. 'Just make sure you do what Mr Crisp says and don't get in the way.'

'I won't, mum,' he said incredulously. 'I always help.'

'I think I'm going to pop and see Carol actually and check on her,' Emma said as she stood up. 'She's not been in the café since the murder, I know she found the body.'

'That's a good idea, love, I'll come with you,' Mum said. 'She was shaken about it yesterday, let's go and see her for a cup of tea.' Mum and Emma spending time together on their own? I wasn't sure what to think about that.

But I didn't have time to worry about it - Noah, Dylan and I were off to carry out the next step of the investigation. It felt like we were getting closer to the truth.

32

Miss Finch had lived in Eastbourne, in a beautiful detached cottage in the affluent Meads area of the town. She had always lived in Eastbourne as far as Dylan could say and driven to wherever she was working. All the academy's schools were close by, so wherever she had worked over the years had never been more than an hour's drive.

Eastbourne was our nearest sizeable town and wasn't too far from Chalk Gap, a few miles along the coast road. Close to our tiny, insular village, but far enough that you could keep your business your own. I envy anyone who gets to enjoy such a luxury.

'I love Eastbourne, we used to live here,' Noah said excitedly from the back of the car, as we admired the beautiful view of the shimmering blue sea on the descent into the town.

'I remember she said once that she'd never work there,' Dylan said. 'She said she wanted her privacy.'

Within two minutes of arriving at Betty Salmon's house, I saw that, if privacy was what she was after, Miss Finch had ended up with the wrong next-door neighbour.

'It's so nice of you to come to tell me in person,' Betty shouted through to Dylan from the kitchen. 'I just can't believe someone would murder Miss Finch. Though you never know what skeletons people have in their closets, do you?'

It amused me that even to her elderly next-door neighbour, completely out of any school context, she was still 'Miss Finch'.

'I always thought she was too good to be true,' Betty said as she carried through a tray with cups of tea. I was too polite to tell her I didn't drink it.

'I wish you'd have let us help you carry that,' Dylan said to her, which I knew would distract from the train of thought she was on. As charming as he was to old ladies like Betty to get them to speak, Dylan maybe wasn't familiar with interviewing people for this purpose - we needed to stay on topic.

'Oh, nonsense, you're guests. I don't have many visitors, I have to make a fuss.'

'Did Miss Finch ever come in for a cup of tea?' I asked.

'Oh no, she thought she was too good for that. Like I said, too good to be true. She was always polite, but I could tell she had a nasty side. Not to speak ill of the dead, of course.'

'Of course,' Dylan was quick to say.

'How did you know she had a nasty side?' Noah asked. I was grateful to have him there. Even if he was still playing detective, he knew the right questions to ask.

'You just know when you come to my age,' she replied. 'Mind you, what I overheard when she was on the phone helped make my mind up. Not that I ever listened in on purpose.'

'Of course you didn't. My mum accidentally overhears things in her pub all the time,' I assured her. It wasn't 'accidentally' in either case. But I wanted to keep Mrs Salmon on side.

'She often took calls in the garden,' she said. 'And if I happen to be out there, I can't help but hear, can I?'

'What did you overhear?' Dylan asked.

'Bits and pieces. She became particularly horrid at that new school of hers, worse than ever. Sacking people, stopping students from coming back, even talking about deporting someone.' She looked at Noah. 'What did you say your name was?'

'I'm Noah.'

'I thought it was. I heard your name a lot.'

'Oh did you, was it good?' Then he seemed to remember. 'I bet it was bad actually. She didn't like me very much.' Sadly, he was right.

I quickly tried to change the subject. 'Did she have many people come to see her at the house?'

'Not really, just that one in the suits with the fancy car.'

'Did he visit often?' I asked.

'Once or twice a week, I think.' Interesting. Maybe mum's theory was right.

Dylan was on the case faster than I was. 'Do you think there was anything romantic going on?'

She looked appalled. 'What? I hope not!'

'Why not? They're not that old.' Noah blurted out. But he wasn't done yet. 'They're nowhere near as old as you.'

'I didn't mean that,' she said, unimpressed. 'The gentleman in the suit, I think you are getting mixed up. The one I'm talking about drives a red Mercedes, Tim, I think his name is.'

'That's the same one,' Dylan confirmed.

'You're definitely mixed up then. He's her brother.'

'WHAT?' Dylan and I both managed at the same time.

'Tim in the suits, yes he's her brother. I think she

might work with him at that new school now, or she did I should say. But he's been coming here for years. Got a young daughter too, but she's not been here for some time. Probably grown up now.'

This little old lady had just turned everything on its head. We were right about there being a secret link between them, but it wasn't a romantic one. Tim Hunt and Miss Finch were brother and sister. I had to wonder why they had kept it quiet at school.

This also meant that their recent argument could be related to their family and perhaps had nothing to do with the school. It made her trying to get rid of him as governor much harsher. Appleby obviously knew this link too and hadn't told me; Tim would presumably have been her next of kin.

'You all seem shocked,' Betty said.

Dylan took this one. 'Yes, we are a bit,' he explained. 'I worked closely with them both and neither of them said anything.'

'Some people are like that, very private. Can't blame them with all the busybodies about. But I've heard them arguing when he's been round too. Terrible row the other week there was. He slammed the door and stormed out, I thought it would come off its hinges!'

'I told you there would be big revelations soon!'

Noah said excitedly.

This was getting more interesting. 'Did you ever see any other family members, apart from Tim and his daughter? No parents or her own children?'

'None, not in the twelve years I've lived next to her. I've tried to get her into a conversation about it a couple of times, but she just cut me off.'

'I've been her PA for 3 years and she was the same with me.'

If we were looking into her personal life for suspects, Tim seemed like the only candidate. But then something struck me.

'Her and Tim have different surnames, that points towards her having a husband,' I said thinking out loud.

'But she's a Miss?' Dylan said.

'She could have just chosen that so students don't question her about her private life,' I said. 'Either that or she took Finch as her professional name.'

'It's funny you say that about Miss and Mrs. I've taken a couple of parcels in for her and had her post by mistake over the years, you know how it is,' she said innocently. 'She's definitely Mrs Finch. I think I've seen another surname on her post too years ago, but I can't remember what now. Although another neighbour might have mentioned something about an ex-husband when she first moved in. But I could be getting her mixed up. It was so long ago.'

'Thank you, Mrs Salmon. Is there anything else you can think of?' Dylan asked, apparently wanting to wrap the conversation up.

I had one more thing to ask. An age old motive in murder mysteries, especially now that we knew one of our suspects was a blood relative. 'Sorry it's delicate, and it's not the kind of thing I'd expect you to know, but do you know anything about her financial situation?'

'Of course!' Noah shouted. 'Did she have much money to inherit?'

Betty laughed. 'I've read quite a few stories where that's the reason people are killed. She must have money behind her because these cottages around here aren't cheap. I could only afford this because of my late husband's pension lump sum.'

'Sorry to hear that,' said Dylan dutifully.

'It's alright. You know it's a shame; me and Miss Finch could have been friends. Two ladies on our own.' She paused and seemed to reflect sadly.

We said our goodbyes and got in the car. On the way back, I summed up the questions our interview had raised.

'Why did they lie about being brother and sister, and what caused the argument?'

'And how much money did she have?' Dylan asked. 'Cos it would presumably all go to Tim if there's no one else. That's a massive motive.'

'I told you, it won't be Mr Hunt - it's too obvious,' Noah insisted. 'Besides, it's not like he's short of a few quid himself.'

'Noah, even Miss Marple said it's always the obvious person who commits the crime.'

'That's rubbish, Sir! In loads of Miss Marples it's not the obvious person – *Murder is Announced, Body in the Library, 4.50 at Paddington* –'

Kat's name flashed up on my screen, saving me. 'Hold that thought,' I said as I answered. 'Hi Kat, you're on speaker, I'm with Dylan in his car. We're on the way back from an interesting –'

'Dylan's driving? Tell him to pull over.' Her voice was impatient and urgent.

'What's wrong?' Dylan asked as he pulled into the lay-by.

'Tim has been found dead at his home. They think he's been murdered.'

'Ah, I told you it wasn't him!' Noah said, sounding overjoyed. 'He was a red herring. He was only there to give us the final twist.'

33

'Edward, I'm doing what I can for you here, mate, help me out. You were the last witness to see him alive.'

It was later that evening and I was at my kitchen table being interviewed by Appleby, which was understandable as I was connected to the scene of a murder.

'I've told you everything I know.' I had, I'd been honest and not left out a single detail.

'You shouldn't know *anything* though, mate. This is exactly why I told you not to go snooping around. Everything's so much more complicated now.'

It was. But depending on the reason (which I still had to establish), Tim was always going to be the next victim of the murderer; his family connection with Miss Finch had caught the killer's attention. Had he worked out who it was? Had he confronted them?

Gracie had left the house before me to go horse

riding and didn't come back until a couple of hours later when she found her dad's body. I wouldn't wish that on anybody. Someone had smashed the back of his head in with an ornament in his living room. That could have easily been done in a fit of anger, but the blow was from behind.

Who did that leave as the murderer, now that Tim was out of the picture? Even though the poisoning was awful, this seemed even more brutal. The ferocity of it made me wonder who could be capable of such an act. Unfortunately, I did this out loud.

'Who do you think it could be then? Did everyone have alibis?' I asked Appleby.

He laughed, a cynical and weary laugh. 'Mate, you don't get this, do you?' He sighed. 'Go on then, I'll humour you. Who do you think it could be?'

I considered the suspects without knowing the alibis. Dylan was completely ruled out as he'd been with either me or my family the entire day.

Kat could have done it at any point after our phone call, and maybe something in our conversation prompted her to visit him. I would say she disliked Tim the most out of everyone left and had the most to gain; her path would probably be clear now to become permanent Head Teacher. I really didn't want to suspect my good friend and housemate, but the options were narrowing.

But if I couldn't imagine Kat being responsible, it was even harder to see Patrick as the killer. He presumably still wasn't speaking to me, and I had no idea where he'd been that day. I still didn't know why he'd lied about seeing Miss Finch the day before the meeting. Was this one of the conversations Dylan overhead? I also remembered Tim commenting to Miss Finch that day as she humiliated Patrick, as if he knew all about it.

My consideration of Gracie as a suspect went back and forth. She had the most connection to the two victims, now that we knew that Miss Finch was her auntie. But could she really have murdered her own dad as well?

The Fletchers seemed to be linked to everything too. Carol found the body. Her insecticide was used to kill Finch. She issued the ID cards, and she told me about the killer using the spare card. And if it wasn't her, she then suspected her husband Brian, who had been responsible for my brother's arrest for the first murder. But what made her think he could be the killer? I was still to find out.

Being none the wiser who it could be, I decided to call Appleby's bluff and see what he knew about the Fletchers. 'I think it was Carol or Brian Fletcher.'

'To be honest, mate, I'm thinking the same thing.' It worked. 'Surprise surprise, their alibi is each other. Are they in it together and trying to throw us off the scent again? He's already tried to put it on your brother. And she seems to be involved in everything. She probably had the most opportunity and knowledge of the school. And it was her poison.'

'Yes, we still need to find out what makes her suspect him,' I agreed.

'Am I going to have to put you in a prison cell to stop you investigating this?' Appleby snapped at me before pausing and letting out a deep breath. 'You're going to do this no matter what I say, aren't you?'

I grinned sheepishly in reply, not making eye contact.

'Okay. If you're just going to have a couple of conversations with your colleagues, then fine. But be careful. The last person you spoke to got murdered.' He paused. 'Just keep in touch with what you find out.'

My former bully had surprised me yet again. Though my mum wasn't convinced when I obeyed my summons to drop into the pub to update her.

'Edward, you're so gullible. It's obviously because he can't solve it himself! Pretending he's doing you a favour; it's to save his own skin. That DCI of his won't be happy now his flash b word mate has been done in. He'll want the murderer found more than ever.'

The flaw in mum's argument was Appleby believing I could solve the murders.

'By the way, I hope he's not trying to put it on Carol – she wasn't in when we knocked for her yesterday, that would have been about the time of the murder.'

'No Mum, he said her and Brian have alibis for each other.' I didn't tell her they were his new prime suspects.

Two of my colleagues had been murdered now, one of whom was my previous prime suspect. I was nowhere near finding the killer; I was out of my depth. Plucky underdog amateur detectives solving murders was the stuff of cozy mystery novels, not real life. A socially awkward librarian who has barely left his hometown was not going to solve this.

Mum had gone to fill in one of the regulars on the latest news, and I was sat at the bar while Alfie worked behind it. I'd been staring into space for a good ten minutes when he came and spoke to me - what he said took me by surprise.

'You okay bro, you seem stressed?' He asked, wiping down a glass with a cloth as he spoke to me.

I *was* stressed. It was all getting too much. 'I don't want any of this,' I replied before blurting out exactly what I was thinking. 'I miss sitting at home, on my own, reading a good book, Alfie.'

He put the glass down hard enough that it made a bang. 'Look, Edward. There's only one reason I'm back behind this bar tonight instead of being behind bars in prison. And there's only one reason Dylan is coming out to his mum as we speak. It's the same reason Noah will be like the new Agatha Christie or whatever. You could be her yourself if you wanted to. And his mum is obviously crazy about you.'

I looked at him but didn't speak, instead I shuffled hesitantly on the bar stool. I've never taken praise well.

'You, Edward. All you. But that's also the only thing that's holding you back. You're your own worst enemy. You could have been a hot-shot detective like Appleby, or you could have been writing your own murder mystery novels. You still could.' He stopped as if he was finished, but then he continued. 'Mum says I'm not meant to talk to you about this stuff but you need to hear it. You had a knockback a few years ago and have ignored your talent since. You're better than working in the school library, Edward. Not that there's anything wrong with that, but you're the most brilliant person I know. You can do anything you want. But for now, go solve this murder.'

I could feel my face burning with embarrassment. 'You think I can?'

'Of course, bro. Mum's right. If Appleby could

solve it, he would have done so by now. He's got all those resources, the swipe records, the alibis, and he's still no clue. He even arrested me just because I was visiting my boyfriend at the school!'

'Secret boyfriend. And you did drop a button at the crime scene,' I pointed out.

'Fair point,' he said and laughed loudly. 'But most of the evidence in this case has turned up because you went out and found it. Not by using fancy police resources, but by good old-fashioned brain power. Now stop feeling sorry for yourself, finish your drink and go and be the hero we all know you are.'

34

It was the next morning, Monday, and I was up early. Usually this is because I've been awake since 4am overthinking something, but this time I'd had a good night's sleep and woken up determined to make progress.

While still lying in bed, I made two separate lists in the notes app on my phone. *My god, I've turned into Noah,* I thought as I reread the first at my kitchen table with my usual orange juice and toast. There were still the alibis and time of death to find out, but I felt that my colleagues' secrets were the key to solving this.

Things I already know that may be significant

- *Miss Finch and Tim were brother and sister and kept the relationship a secret.*
- *They had a fallout, and she tried to get rid of him as Chair of Governors.*
- *Dylan could not have killed Tim.*
- *Motives - Miss Finch had sacked Brian, tried to sack Gracie's dad, had taken the job Kat*

wanted, threatened to sack Patrick (more to story – see below).

- *The killer used the spare ID card, accessed Carol's insecticide and turned off CCTV, then put poison in the water dispenser.*
- *The killer entered Tim's home and struck him over the head from behind.*

Things I need to find out

- *The missing part of Patrick's story – why he didn't tell me he saw Miss Finch the day before the meeting, and what was said?*
- *The real reason Carol suspects her own husband – she may know something she hasn't told anyone.*
- *The reason why Miss Finch and Tim argued and why she tried to get rid of him.*
- *Possibly related to this - the secret Gracie referred to. Could just be that they were brother/sister, or might be something else.*
- *Whether Kat knew they were brother and sister, and whether she's implicated in any other part of the case.*

Looking closely at the second list, I knew the answer lay in at least one of those points. It seemed strange to me it had only been two days since Miss Finch had been murdered. My brother was right, I had found out a lot already and Appleby had told me what I needed to do next. I had to talk to each of my colleagues. Poirot often said that the answer lay in conversation; that all murderers love to talk and will eventually give themselves away.

I got the chance to speak to the first one when Kat appeared in the kitchen in her usual fluffy pink dressing gown. I was focusing on the list on my phone and didn't notice her come in at first.

'Morning Ed, are you studying your case notes?'

'Something like that,' I replied. I didn't mention they included her.

'Ed, who would kill both Anne and Tim?' she asked as she flicked the switch on the kettle and pottered around preparing her tea. 'Do you think they're going to kill again?'

'I don't think so,' I mused. 'Someone set out to kill Miss Finch, and now we've learned that Tim was her brother. I don't think anyone else is in danger; Appleby said Gracie will be safe with the foster family they've put her with.' I had convinced myself of this and desperately hoped that I was right.

'I still can't believe that. Why did they keep it a secret?'

I thought she might have known this already and told her just that.

'I would have told you if I did,' she said quickly. 'I just don't understand why he didn't say it was his sister who was the new Head. Maybe so they weren't accused of nepotism?'

'Maybe, but they didn't hide the fact they knew each other. Dylan confirmed that too.' I decided to ask her something I had been wondering.

'Do you think you'll become Head permanently?'

She stopped what she was doing and turned to face me, empty cup in hand. 'Now Tim's not around to oppose it, you mean?'

I looked away. I did mean that. I was trying to stay confident talking to people about the case, but I panicked at getting caught out. 'That's not... I meant...'

'It's okay. I'm not going to fly off at you like Patrick.' She knew about that? I'd still not even seen Patrick since then; he'd stayed out of my way. 'I'm not against your whole Hercule Poirot thing. You're probably the best person to solve this before anything else bad happens. And I know you've got to consider everyone now - there's not many of us left under suspicion.'

'Just me, you, Carol, Gracie and Patrick who have access,' I confirmed. 'And Brian or anyone else could easily have got in.'

'Oh yes, Dylan's in the clear now, isn't he? He couldn't have killed Tim.'

'On the assumption the same person killed them both, yes.' I had considered this. It was possible there were two separate killers, or that Dylan had an accomplice, but it seemed unlikely at this point.

'I'm pleased it's definitely not Dylan,' she remarked as she sat down to join me.

'Did you think it might be?' I was surprised at this.

'I don't know. Not really. We get on well, but I've only known him for a few months. I'm working off the idea this is so horrific it must be someone I don't know very well.'

That was an interesting perspective. As a really people-focused Deputy Head, Kat had always made sure she knew everyone professionally, if not personally. I was intrigued by this, but her earlier mention of Patrick had set off a wave of anxiety in me I was struggling to shake. I had to ask her.

'What did Patrick say to you then?' I attempted to ask casually.

'He's mad at you, but he will be fine,' she replied. 'He just doesn't like being caught up in all this, I think he feels exposed.'

It was true, Patrick had been my best friend for nearly 12 years and in all that time he had remained a laid-back, worry-free guy. Yes, he got into scrapes like having trouble with girlfriends or chatting up the wrong person, and I'd seen him get angry watching football, but he seemed to go through life showing no deeper worries. But did that mean he didn't have them?

'I know I upset him by questioning him again, there was just something not quite right,' I explained. 'You heard Miss Finch in the meeting refer to seeing him the previous day, but he claimed not to have seen her since before the holidays.'

'I probably shouldn't say,' she began, which is always the start of something significant. 'But I was in work that day and he *was* there for a meeting with her.'

'So why has he lied about it? What hasn't he told me?' I thought out loud.

'I don't know, Edward. All I know is that it was something to do with the visa stuff and it didn't go well. He looked so upset when he walked past my office window. I remember thinking that he didn't just look angry, he looked crushed.'

'But he'd sorted the visa,' I said. 'It was just that his contract was tied to it, so she was threatening to get rid of him if he didn't do what she wanted.'

'It seemed more than that,' she replied as she sipped her tea.

'I don't know, he's been there eight years and his job is important to him. He was worried about it before the summer.'

'You should have seen him though,' she said. 'It just seemed more personal than that.'

'But what, though? What's more important to him than his job?' I stopped, interrupted by my train of thought.

'What?' Kat asked.

'Is he in the house?' I asked as I stood up from the table, ready for action.

'No, he was going to the old school site to sort stuff he needs to take to the new building.' We still weren't allowed in the new building as it was a crime scene, but we could go to the old building across the village.

'I need to see him,' I called out as I rushed away from the kitchen. 'I think I've worked out what Finch threatened him with.'

35

Sure enough, I found Patrick sorting his students' work in his classroom at the old site. Each student had their own drawer, and he appeared to be looking through them and deciding what to keep, but there must have been at least fifty piles of paper around him. It was utter chaos and typical of my unorganised friend.

He looked around as he sensed me at his classroom door. Was he even going to speak to me?

'At least you're not having a barbecue this time.' I attempted a joke as I surveyed the mass of paper around me. 'What about a bonfire instead?'

'Some of this work, that's the best place for it,' he laughed. 'I don't know what kind of clown their English teacher is.'

'One who is owed an apology,' I said.

'No, buddy. I'm sorry. It's not you,' he said as he sat down and pulled out a chair for me to do the same. 'I should never have stormed off like that. People have been killed, we're all going to question each other. Your brother was falsely arrested and your childhood enemy is leading the case. I think you're entitled to look around a bit.'

'I still don't know who it is,' I admitted, 'but I trust you. I know it's not you.'

'No, it's not,' he said. 'But I did lie to you.' An admission - we were getting somewhere.

'I know you did. And it's fine. I know why.'

'You do?' he seemed surprised.

'Yes. When you went missing and went to London and then the airport, you weren't on your own, were you?'

He looked even more shocked, but then he started grinning. 'You really are an excellent detective, buddy. How did you know?'

'Patrick, I know you,' I said honestly. 'I've known you for twelve years and you've always been there for me. You befriended a friendless loner at uni and have kept me under your wing ever since.'

'Don't say that, Edward.'

'It's fine, it's true. You even helped me through my breakdown.'

I felt the words heavy in the air. I didn't say that word out loud very often. And this is the first time I've directly mentioned it in this account. But it's true, I went through a bad patch a while back. I don't even know why – life is just hard sometimes, especially when it doesn't turn out how you were hoping. I almost didn't recover, but my brilliant friend Patrick is one of the reasons I did.

'Edward, it's okay, you don't have to say it.'

I felt self-conscious, but I had to power through it and say what I needed to say.

'I do. You even moved me in with you and Kat to help me. But I've realised, in twelve years of knowing you, you've needed nothing in return.'

'You know me, buddy, I don't worry about things.'

'But you do, we all do. Just because you act happy and laid back all the time, it doesn't mean you don't have worries. I bottled everything up and it led me to a breakdown.' That word again. I pressed on. 'The thing I'm trying to say is, you could have told me and I'd have helped you figure it out.'

'Told you what?'

'That your mum is in this country illegally. And that Miss Finch was blackmailing you about it.'

He looked relieved I'd said it. 'How did you know?'

'I pieced it together from a few different things.'

I knew he'd lied about the day before the staff meeting, but I didn't know why. He'd already surprised me earlier with the story about his heritage, and I couldn't work out why he had never told me, even after his 'right to remain' was sorted out.

All of this pointed to it still being related to his immigration status, but I didn't know how. When Kat told me about his reaction when he left Miss Finch, and about how personal it looked, I realised the only person he was close enough to to be upset about like that was his mum. Combined with his panicked airport visit and what I was getting to know about Miss Finch's personality, my theory was that she'd found out Patrick's mum was here illegally and she'd revealed that the day before the meeting.

'She rang me and said I had to come and see her, that it was in my best interests. I was so shocked that she'd gone to the trouble of finding out. Who does that?' He tore the edges of one of the scrap pieces of paper in front of him.

Without disrespecting the dead, I'd learned that Miss Finch was exactly the sort of person who does that, and worse besides.

'And for what?' he continued, fiddling with the paper still. 'Just to get me to take a pay cut and do a few extra duties. I think she enjoyed controlling people. So I showed her at that staff meeting she couldn't control me.'

'But she tore you down in front of us all.'

'Sadly, yeah. She told me that if I said anything,

she'd say way worse about me and that Tim would back her up.' The paper in his hand was now screwed up in a ball and he threw it across the room. 'I didn't take her seriously, but as soon as she mentioned my 'unprofessional behaviour' in front of you all, I realised I'd made a mistake.'

I looked at the floor where the paper ball landed. 'No wonder you were so upset when I saw you on the beach.'

'My head was all over the place. I went to Brighton and told my mum, and we decided we had to sort out her residency or make a run for it back to Spain.'

'What happened next?' I asked as I walked across to pick up the paper ball and put it in the bin.

'I stayed at her house that night and she packed all her stuff. We got up at 5am the next morning and drove to ours to get my stuff while you and Kat were still asleep. Then we drove to London first to try the Embassy to have one last go to sort it out, but nerves got the better of us while we were queuing, so we went to Gatwick ready to leave.'

'Patrick, that's awful.'

He continued. 'I ignored my phone for hours because I didn't want to deal with everyone asking where I was, but, when I finally looked, I saw all the messages about Miss Finch being found dead.

We knew then we couldn't leave. It would look like I was guilty and running from the murder, and my mum would have been dragged into it anyway.'

'And there was maybe no need to go if Miss Finch was dead.'

'Maybe. It sounds awful saying it, doesn't it?' He said sombrely. This was the most open and frank I'd ever seen carefree Patrick. 'But to be honest, mate, it was a reality check. Running away wasn't the answer. We need to sort it out. It's just some stupid paperwork thing – obviously my dad was Spanish and mum's his widow. They allow EU citizens who are already here residency so we're going to go to the Embassy again tomorrow and try to sort it out.'

I took all of this in, and then something occurred to me. 'Do you think Tim knew about this?'

'Probably, they seemed to be in everything together. Still can't believe they're brother and sister. But that's the other thing, I was on my own all day yesterday, so I've no alibi except being logged into my PlayStation playing FIFA. I'm expecting Appleby to pull me in again any moment, and I don't want my mum involved.'

'You should be okay for now, he thinks it's one or both of the Fletchers.'

'It's mad isn't it, to think someone we know

killed two people.'

'I know. I'm still not sure it's them, but there's only them, Kat and Gracie left.'

'There's no way it's Kat, buddy,' he said adamantly, almost aggressively. I wondered sometimes if there was still something between them. He paused for a moment before speaking again in a much different tone. 'You know there's that Agatha Christie one where the kid did it, don't you?'

How many times was I going to hear this? 'You mean it could be Gracie? You sound like Noah!'

'I've taught him for five years, buddy, I've heard that a hundred times.'

'What do you think?'

'Poor kid. No, I don't think it's going to be her. But I'll tell you this, mate, I spoke to Kat about it yesterday. After what I saw of Miss Finch, there will be more to her argument with Tim than you think. Not to speak ill of the dead, but she was a nasty piece of work.'

I thought about this. 'I need to speak to Gracie, but I'll have to do it sensitively, she lost her dad yesterday. But I'm going to try to speak to Carol first if she's here.'

'Bad luck, Edward,' he said, glancing over to his classroom window facing the old school entrance. 'I saw her rush out of the gates a couple of minutes after you walked through them.'

'She's avoiding me.'

'Everyone's been avoiding you, they're terrified what you'll find out next,' he quipped. 'You're like Mr Marple these days.'

'Hilarious. I just need to know what Carol's not telling me.'

36

As I walked the couple of minutes from the old site to Carol's house, I updated my phone with what I now knew from my first list.

- *~~The missing part of Patrick's story – why he didn't tell me he saw Miss Finch the day before the meeting, and what was said~~*
- *The real reason Carol suspects Brian, her own husband – she may know something she hasn't told anyone*
- *The reason Miss Finch and Tim argued and why she tried to get rid of him*
- *Maybe related to this - the secret Gracie referred to. Could just be that they were brother/sister, or might be something else*
- *~~If Kat knew they were brother and sister, and if she has any bearing on anything else in the case~~*

In a moment, I would hopefully be able to get to the bottom of things with Carol. But as I was about to turn into their road, my brother rang.

'Edward, didn't you say you needed to speak to that teenage girl who rides the horse, Tim Hunt's daughter?'

'Yes, why?'

'I can see her from the pub window. She's sat on the bench across the village square, engrossed in her phone. I'll tell you if she goes anywhere, but she's been here a few minutes. You should catch her if you hurry up,'

'Cheers, Alfie, I'm on the way.' I ended the call and glanced across at Carol and Brian's house. This could be my only chance to speak to Gracie. They would have to wait.

To say I'm not athletic is an understatement. I don't run often, but I put all my effort into sprinting up West Chalk Road and onto the high street. By the time I reached the village square, I had a stitch, was holding my side and could barely breathe. Luckily, Gracie was still sat on the bench as I panted my way over to her.

'What on earth has happened to you?' she said as she stared at me with utter disdain.

'I'm so sorry about your dad, Gracie.' I tried to catch my breath.

'I think you should be more sorry for yourself. You're going to be joining him by the looks of it,' she said without missing a beat. An odd thing to say, but she was a grieving teenager, and she was already outspoken even before this loss.

'I suppose you better sit down before you collapse,' she said, gesturing to the space next to her.

'You probably want to know why I'm out of breath like this,' I panted as I sat down.

'I already know. Your brother in the window over there saw me, so you legged it over here as quick as you could to speak to me.' She smiled smugly. 'See, you're not the only detective round here.'

'Ah, you spotted him, did you?'

'Spotted him? He's not moved from the window for the last 10 minutes. If I didn't know he was gay, I'd have thought he was perving on me.' She was particularly sharp today, understandably.

'So you're still in the village?'

'Yeah, they've put me with some crappy foster family while they try to get hold of my mum. Not that I want to live with her either.' I glanced at her as she paused.

'I can't even imagine what you're going through.'

'You don't know the half of it, Sir.' I don't think I'd ever heard Gracie call me 'Sir' in the entire time I'd been at the school. She inhaled noisily, and I felt there was more she wanted to say.

Finally she spoke again. 'Find out, Sir. Find out who killed my dad. Please.'

'I will, Gracie, that's what I'm trying to do. And your auntie.' She looked in surprise. 'I only found out about that connection yesterday.'

'I don't care about her, I hope she rots. It's all her fault.'

'What is, your dad's murder?'

'Probably.' She stopped again. 'But something else too.'

'Something else you want to tell me?'

'I don't know.'

'If I don't know, I can't help. And you said you want me to solve the murder, it might be important. Besides, it looks like you could do with someone to talk to.'

'Maybe.' I saw a scared young girl who genuinely didn't know what to do.

And then she spoke again. 'I'm pregnant.'

I don't know exactly what I expected her to say, but it wasn't that.

Gracie seemed to take my surprise for disgust. 'I know what you're thinking. Don't worry, me and Dad had it all from my lovely auntie.'

Ah, so this was the link to Miss Finch. 'Wasn't she supportive?'

'Supportive, are you joking? She pretended she wasn't related to us even before this. When she found out, she told my dad I had to get rid of it or I wasn't welcome at the sixth form to do my A Levels.'

'But Gracie, you're an excellent student.'

'Tell me about it, I wish someone had told *her* that before she died. My dad tried to stick up for me and they had a massive row about it. She tried to get rid of him from the school. Her own family. How could she?'

She looked down at the ground, her speech over for now. So this was the argument between Miss Finch and Tim. No wonder it had turned so nasty.

'But why did she feel so strongly about it?'

'I don't know, stupid old cow. My dad said it's something to do with her past. She had a kid herself or something with her husband, but there was some big fall out. Her husband died, but apparently they'd split up before that and the kid was on his side. So no one can have a kid ever cos she doesn't speak to hers?'

'What made them fall out?'

'Dunno, this was before I was born. Dad is always secretive about it, I'm not even meant to know. Like I care anyway. It's too late now, him and my auntie are both dead.'

So our speculation was right, Miss Finch had a husband – or rather an ex-husband, and a past she'd left behind. I had no idea how all of this linked to the murders, or if it even did.

As I thought about this, Gracie started crying quietly beside me. I got out my phone and typed into it quickly. Trying to find out what I could about Miss Finch would have to wait. A traumatised girl was going through more than she ever should, and she needed advice and support. I wasn't the best placed to do that myself, but I had an idea who could. A moment later, I saw my brother give a thumbs up from the window.

As you've probably gathered by now, my mum can be a pain sometimes, but she knows exactly what to do in situations like this. Seemingly within seconds, I saw her fly out of the pub and race across the square towards us. She was in far better shape than I was.

Gracie glanced up as my mum gently sat down on the other side of the bench from me.

'I'm Edward's mother,' she said by way of explanation. I don't quite know why it happened, but, on hearing this, Gracie's gentle cry broke into a sob and she collapsed onto my mum's shoulder. 'It's alright love, we'll work something out for you.'

She let her cry like that for what seemed like forever, but in reality it was only a minute. As

Gracie's cries subsided a little, Mum slowly stood up with her arm still around her. 'Come on love, let's go in the pub and get a nice cup of tea.' Mum nodded at me as she led Gracie away.

I watched them head into the pub. I felt overwhelmed and out of my depth; Gracie's situation was heart-breaking and I was no closer to solving anything. I could feel the panic rising in me. Before I knew it, I found myself across the square in Emma's café. I focused on my breathing and keeping calm as I relayed the tale about Gracie (not mentioning the pregnancy, it wasn't my place).

'How is she?' Emma asked, stopping wiping down a table and coming to sit down.

'Messed up," I replied. 'She's got a lot to get through.'

'It was nice of you to get your mum to look after her. You're a good man, Edward.'

At this moment, with chaos around me and not seeing that I'd got any closer to working things out, I didn't feel it.

'But what good is that? Everyone always says what a nice guy I am, but so what? Two people are dead, the police are useless and everyone thinks I should be able to solve it - just because I have a thing for old detective novels and everyone assumes I'm smart.' I didn't know where that came from. Alfie had given me a pep talk only the night before, telling me I could solve this, but my confidence never lasts long.

'Edward, you *are* smart.' She put her hand on my arm.

'Emma, who are we kidding? I'm a 32-year-old school librarian, with crippling anxiety, who's barely left the village because I'm so afraid of what's out there. I haven't even got the guts to do anything with a novel I finished writing ten years ago, even though it might be good enough to do quite well. And I've got my brother telling me to solve this murder – but what if I can't?'

'Then if you can't, you can't, she said calmly. 'It's nothing to be ashamed of, it's literally the police's job and they haven't been able to either.'

She was right. 'I'm sorry. I just felt like we were so close when we found out that Tim was her brother – I was convinced it was him. But now he's dead too, and maybe I could have prevented it. I think I just need to stick to fictional murders and leave it to the police.'

'Have you got anyone else you still need to talk to?'

'Yes, Carol.'

'Carol, really?' She seemed surprised, but anyone we knew would be a surprise. 'I am worried about her, actually. She wasn't in when me and your

Mum went to see her, she's still not been in the café and she's not replied to my messages. You don't think it's her, do you?'

I didn't want to give too much away, or implicate our friends and neighbours. 'I don't know, there's just one last thing to check with her. But maybe it's not worth it.'

'It's up to you Edward, you've come this far.' Her hand on my arm went down to hold my hand. 'If you see her, tell her to come in the café and see me later. Or, if not, I'll pop round after work – I want to check she's alright.' The way Emma ran the café reminded me of Mum; a regular customer goes missing for a day and she sends out a search party.

As we said our goodbyes, she leaned forward suddenly and kissed me on the cheek. 'I believe in you, and lots of people do – even if you don't believe in yourself.'

I headed back across the square when I saw Brian Fletcher arrive at the pub. It was barely lunchtime, this was early even for him. He probably wanted to get away from Carol if she was still suspicious of him over the case. But it was perfect for me, as Carol would be on her own at home. Maybe Emma was right – I just needed to believe in myself. I glanced again at my list and updated it following my conversation with Gracie.

- ~~*The missing part of Patrick's story – why*~~

~~*he didn't tell me he saw Miss Finch the day before the meeting, and what was said*~~

- *The real reason Carol suspects Brian, her own husband – she may know something she hasn't told anyone*
- ~~*The reason Miss Finch and Tim argued and why she tried to get rid of him*~~
- ~~*Maybe related to this – the secret Gracie referred to. Could just be that they were brother/sister, or might be something else*~~
- ~~*If Kat knew they were brother and sister, and if she has any bearing on anything else in the case*~~

Almost every question had been answered, and it hadn't brought me to the truth. There was only one left now, and I was about to find out what Carol had been hiding.

37

'Sorry Edward, I can't speak right now.'

As soon as Carol saw it was me, she shut the door again as quickly as she could. I wasn't fast enough to stop her.

'Come on, Carol, just let me in so we can talk.'

'Go away, Edward!'

'I can help you.'

'I said go away!'

One of her neighbours opened their door for a second and glanced around the mews, pretending they were looking for someone. It would be around Chalk Gap within minutes that I was Carol's jilted toy boy.

'Carol...' I stopped as I heard a thump on the other side of the door. She had thrown herself back to rest against it. I knew what would get her to open the door – the truth.

'Carol, I know why you're suspicious of Brian. You had the spare ID at home as well as your own, didn't you? And it went missing the night before Miss Finch's death. You think Brian stole it.'

After a second, the door opened, and Carol stood opposite me. As soon as I saw her face, I could tell I was right.

I followed her in and sat down in the lounge, glancing again at the celebrity chef books as 'live laugh love' sat above me. She seemed reluctant to tell me at first, but, slowly, she opened up.

'Okay, yes, I had the spare ID card at home. Almost all the staff live in the village, and they all know where we live – so it made sense.'

'And Brian knew about this?'

She exhaled and fidgeted with her hands. 'Yes, he did. But if you remember me telling you, I'd only sorted out the swipe cards that day, so the spare was still in my bag.'

'But it went missing?'

She nodded her head. 'After I dragged Brian out of the pub and we'd had our falling out, I heard him banging around downstairs and the door shutting. The next morning I checked my bag, and it wasn't there anymore. I looked everywhere for it, that's why I was so late getting to school when I found her – I should have been there at 7.'

Her story seemed to finally explain what happened. 'So you think he took it?'

'I don't know, Edward love – he was furious when I asked him. He said ordinary blokes don't turn into psycho killers just because they got sacked. But I just can't stop thinking... what if it's him?' She finally broke down in tears, putting her head in her hands so I wouldn't see.

I'm so uncomfortable seeing people upset, but it seemed to be a regular occurrence at the moment. I didn't have Mum a few metres away this time to come and save the day, so we sat in silence for a moment.

'He was even out yesterday afternoon when Tim was killed,' she added in a muffled, teary voice through her hands. 'We told the DI that we were together, but we weren't – not at first. He said he went fishing.'

'And wasn't he?'

'Well, yes. I was worried about where he was so I drove to Cuckmere river and sure enough, there he was. But he could have been to Tim's before.'

'Yes, I suppose he could have,' I replied.

As she'd been telling me this story, I received a call from Kat which I diverted. But immediately after I also got a message from her - '*Come to old school site NOW. Urgent. You have to see this ASAP!*'

Then I got a missed call, followed by another text message, this time from Patrick.

'Buddy why aren't you answering Kat? I'm with her. Whatever you're doing, drop it. We've found something and we know who the murderer is.'

38

MURDER IN THE WATER BY NOAH OXLEY

(Reprint of the last page from *Chapter 30: The Final Showdown*)

All the suspects sat in the classroom, hanging on the brilliant teenage detective's every word. Usually he was the one sat listening to the teachers talk at the front, but the situation had been reversed, he was the one doing the talking now. It was the only way they would ever find out who had killed their boss, the Head Teacher. He had eliminated most suspects already, but not before sharing each of their real secrets.

But now it was time. Time to find out who had poisoned Mrs Macaw's water dispenser. As well as the suspects, the know-it-all Detective Inspector and two of her officers stood by. They'd be needed in a minute.

He came to Mr Twist, the school caretaker. His wife, the sacked Science teacher Mrs Twist, sat nervously next to him.

'Mr Twist, could you please show everyone your set of school keys?'

'Erm yes, I guess,' the caretaker said as he took them out of his pocket for all to see.

'Thank you. And now can you show us your spare set?'

The caretaker looked panicked. 'What spare set?'

'Please don't play dumb with me,' the incredible young detective said confidently. 'I know you have two sets of keys to the school.'

'The other set is at home,' the anxious caretaker said.

'Lies!' the detective declared. 'You've lost them, haven't you? Since the night before the murder.'

Mr Twist didn't dare look up. He had been caught out.

'And now,' said the detective, turning to the caretaker's sacked wife, 'Mrs Twist, could you please take the spare keys out of your handbag?'

'What keys? I don't have them.' She looked genuinely scared as she answered.

'More lies!' said the fantastic detective.

'I'm not lying, I'll show you,' she said as she reached into her bag. To everyone's shock, she lifted out an identical set of keys. 'But wait, I didn't put these

there. These aren't mine!'

'No, they aren't yours, you stole them,' the detective said brilliantly. He looked at the two officers. 'Arrest her, boys.'

The DI, looking so impressed, gave the nod to her officers who came and handcuffed Mrs Twist.

'But I'm innocent! I've been set up!' the disgraced ex-teacher shouted as they led her out of the room.

'That's what they all say,' the young prodigy detective said to her. 'Tell it to the jury. Case closed!'

Everyone left the room, leaving the youthful detective to bask in his own brilliance. He had put on quite a show, just like he wanted. Just like his hero, Hercule Poirot. All loose ends were tied up and justice had been done.

At least that's what everyone was supposed to think. It had been so easy to get Mr Twist's spare keys from him when he wasn't looking. And even easier to plant them in Mrs Twist's bag after the murder.

And it was easier still to trick Mr Twist into talking about the products in his caretaker's cupboard, so that the young genius had known exactly what to steal to poison Mrs Macaw.

Now everyone would think the sacked teacher had killed her in revenge, while the brilliant brain had pulled off the perfect crime. And he would do it again too – 'solving' every crime that he actually committed. He really would become the best detective in the world.

39

I looked in disbelief at Kat and Patrick as I finished reading.

So this was the final and most damning clue, the one I'd not expected. But it linked the case together and, sadly, I could now see everything clearly. It was the last outcome I'd ever imagined.

'I just can't believe it's him, mate,' Patrick said. 'All the times he told me about Christie's twist where the kid was the killer. It's like he was trolling me the entire time, wanting me to know what he had planned. He just combined it with the other famous twist where the narrator did it.'

Now wasn't the time to correct Patrick and tell him it technically wasn't the narrator as it was written in third person.

'But they weren't the only twists,' I said. 'He told me it would be one that had never been done before. And it hasn't, as far as I know. The detective being the real killer each time and framing someone else for it.'

'Not much of a twist after the first book,' Kat commented.

'It was the novel project I was telling you about, I was hoping I'd find a copy here,' Patrick clarified. 'It was just a fun exercise to build their writing skills before the exam, I never got to read the end.'

'And he would have kept another copy for himself?' I asked.

'Oh yes, I remember him printing it off to take home and how proud he was.'

'So we're all agreed he must have done it then?' Kat asked.

No, not Noah, surely not. If the two people presenting this to me weren't my best friends, I'd even consider this being a forgery to set him up. I knew it wasn't, but this didn't fit in with the conclusions I'd come to while listening to Carol.

'Of course he must have,' Patrick said. 'Apart from a couple of gender reverses, this is written pretty much exactly how the murder happened – months before it did.'

'Yes, I suppose it can't be a coincidence,' she replied. I did hear the two of them, but I wasn't really listening. I was deep in thought.

'And, Edward, didn't he say to you it would be amazing if Miss Finch became a murder victim on the launch day?' Patrick asked.

I nodded, shook from my trance. 'He did, but afterwards he was worried people would think it was him because he predicted it. Come to think of it, it was when he was talking about his book – he must have been scared it would point to him.'

'Well, of course he was,' Patrick said. 'That's because it does point to him. What do you want to do, Edward?'

I said nothing in reply.

'I suppose we should ring DI Appleby,' Kat said sadly.

'Not yet,' I said. 'Let me speak to his mum first.'

'Fair enough, buddy,' Patrick said. 'I know you're getting close to her and he's only a kid. It seems right that you tell her before we turn him in.'

And so it was with a heavy heart that I arrived at the café that afternoon. There was an old lady sipping her tea in the corner, but I told Emma I needed to speak to her urgently as soon as the lady left. A few minutes later, Emma saw her out and put the 'closed' sign on the door behind her. She came and sat down without saying a word.

'You know why I'm here, don't you?'

She nodded without looking at me. I took a breath. This would be the hardest conversation of my life.

'Did you read the end of Noah's novel?'

She nodded again, but still couldn't look at me. She knew what I was about to say would tear her apart from her son.

'Emma,' I started. 'You killed Miss Finch, didn't you?'

40

We sat in silence for a while before she spoke. 'How do you know it's me?'

It centred around the spare ID Carol had. Appleby confirmed this was the ID used to access the scene, and Carol finally admitted she had the keys but lost them. There was a chance Carol was lying, but I knew she wasn't. Over the last couple of days, I could tell she was genuinely worried and upset and it seemed to be linked to Brian. But could Brian, as drunk as he was that night, have got away with stealing the ID, taking and planting the poison, then removing the CCTV? It didn't feel right – it felt more like pre-mediation than drunken rage.

But if not the Fletchers, then who? Most other suspects had been pretty much eliminated, and I'd never been comfortable with it being someone I knew well. As I'd listened to Carol's story, I thought - was there anyone else who'd have the knowledge to carry out the murder and the opportunity to steal Carol's ID? Then I had a sudden thought. A thought that tore right through me, but one that made sense.

Emma. The same Emma who'd been sat at the next table when Carol put her bag down in the pub. But that was just my instinct. She was right – how did I know?

'My friends found Noah's book in the old school building and the ending made them think it was him. It threw me for a moment, but then I realised – you read it and got the inspiration for the whole idea. You realised that murder mystery plots, which Noah loves, could be applied to real life.'

'I didn't even know there was a copy at school, I thought I had the only one.'

'Which I bet is nowhere to be found. I double checked with Patrick that Noah took a copy home before summer, but I knew he was going to say yes. From there, it would be so easy to find out what you needed from Carol every time she came to the café. Do you know Carol even suspected Noah when we first found the body, when she saw him outside?'

'He wasn't meant to be there that day,' she said with anger in her voice.

'I know, but because he was, and seemed so thrilled with the murder, she thought he must have been listening in to her conversations with you and carried it out. She didn't realise she was helping the actual murderer herself, face to face.'

'Okay, and then what?' She sat back and folded her arms, looking at me in defiance.

'All you had to do then was find the opportunity to get the spare ID. When Carol still hadn't issued the IDs by the day before, you dropped Noah off at school that day to try again to get one. That's why Finch was so angry about Noah being there – she must have seen you.'

'Why would she be angry at seeing me?' She'd unfolded her arms and drummed her fingers impatiently on the table.

'I'll come back to that,' I replied, having planned what I would say carefully. 'But you finally got your opportunity for your plan on Friday night. It would have only taken a moment to take Carol's spare ID from her bag once you knew Brian was drunk enough to provide a distraction – I'd wondered why Carol had turned up. You were occupied with your phone before I sat with you; you were texting her, weren't you?'

'It sounds like you know everything,' she said, rolling her eyes. The sweet, upbeat woman I'd been getting to know had vanished.

'That's not all though. I remembered when Brian was getting thrown off stage he shouted 'cheers for the drinks, love.' At the time I thought it was to Mum on the bar, but when I thought about it earlier I realised - she wasn't even there then, she was on a break. You were buying him drinks to get him drunk enough for Carol to come, weren't you?"

She said nothing this time, she just looked at the floor.

'And then you chatted to me enough to have an alibi for a good portion of the night. You know my Mum and her gossip well enough to know a budding romance with me would be the talk of the village; no one would even realise or take notice of the time you left. Just that you were sat with me most of the night.'

'That's not fair, Edward,' she said, raising her head and looking straight at me. 'And it's not true. I really liked you.'

I ignored this and carried on. 'You've already told me where your plan first went wrong - Noah wasn't supposed to be at school the morning Carol found the body. That's why you were so worried when we returned that day. Your next problem was Carol not going in the café after the murder, so you could plant the keys back on her for Brian to get the blame. You tried messaging her, you even tried going to see her – but Mum gate-crashed that and Carol wasn't in anyway.

'Time was running out to plant the keys back, so you came up with the idea to frame Tim. At the dinner, you heard he was falling under suspicion, so he was the perfect person. Once you left Mum, you went straight to Tim's house to plant the keys on him. You probably guessed there was a good chance Finch's neighbour would know Tim was her brother, so that would put him even more in the frame. And it was perfect. Again, I'll come back to how you knew that.

'But something must have gone wrong, most likely Tim guessing what you were trying to do, or catching you. I imagine he threatened to expose you there and then. Running out of options, you struck him with the ornament in desperation.'

She sat forward, leaning her hands on the table now, and looked straight in my eyes. 'Isn't this meant to be done in a big dramatic reveal in a room full of people? You're not even following the classic mystery tropes. I'm disappointed.'

'Poirot sometimes did a one-on-one confrontation with the killer,' I batted straight back. 'More importantly, I wouldn't do that to Noah.'

She turned away, looking ashamed for the first time. She composed herself and returned her gaze to me. 'So, go on, how did Finch know me when I dropped Noah off? And how would I know Tim was her brother before you did?'

This was something I'd only just worked out. After realising Emma had the opportunity to steal Carol's spare ID and commit both murders, I was struggling to link it to a motive. Miss Finch had tried to stop Noah from continuing on after school, and any protective parent would be angry about that. But enough to murder? It seemed more personal. I sat back and thought about everything from the last few days, trying to piece together what I knew and link it to Emma. Then I did.

'You're Miss Finch's estranged daughter.'

For the first time in our conversation, she looked shocked. I don't know if she expected me to work that part out, though she'd previously told me she believed in me. But that, like most of our budding relationship, could have been a lie.

'Tell me how you know that.'

'A few things had led me to it. Gracie told me Miss Finch had an adult child she'd argued with and didn't speak to. I knew Finch was from Eastbourne, so it occurred to me that the son or daughter (Gracie didn't confirm which) may still be around. Once I suspected you, it came into my head – what if you're the daughter? Then everything else fitted into place.'

'Like what?'

'Things that might not seem relevant separately all fit together. First, Noah said on the way to Eastbourne you used to live there. And you mentioned your dad several times, but never your mum; you even said it was just you and Noah after he died. Then - and I said I'd come back to this

- the way Finch was so rattled about Noah being in school the day before, more than she usually is about school issues. It was because she saw you.

'And finally, we're the same age which means you had Noah at 15 or 16. About the right age for someone as Draconian as Finch to disown you for it.' Like she was disowning Gracie for doing the same thing at a similar age, I thought to myself – but it wasn't my place to tell Emma that.

I got to the end of my theories and was met with silence again. She'd nodded in all the right places, and I knew this was what had happened. I'd worked out how and the secret connection between murderer and victim, but there was still a part of the story missing.

Whenever I work out who the killer is in murder mysteries I read, it's usually because I spot *how* they did it: the lie they told, the discrepancy in their story, the identity they'd hidden. But I struggled more with the *why*. What would bring one human being to kill another?

'Why?' I asked her. 'Why did you do it?' I knew that Emma was Miss Finch's estranged daughter with no love lost, but not what drove her to murder.

There was yet another silence before Emma finally spoke, slowly and quietly, with the energy drained from her voice.

'She was a control freak. She wanted to make up with me, but on her own terms. I hadn't seen her for over 15 years when she walked into the café to see me last year. Tim had told her we'd moved to Chalk Gap, and that I was running the café.

'I didn't even know he lived here at first, but then he started coming in here regularly. He always asked how I was, but that was it. He told me he'd become a governor at Noah and Gracie's school. Then he started trying to have longer conversations, and eventually he mentioned my mother. I told him I wasn't interested, and he apologised for bringing it up, but then it fell into a pattern. Every couple of months, he'd bring up my mother as he bought his coffee, and I said again I didn't want to know. This was for about a year until one day she just walked in to see me.'

'What happened?' I was addressing a killer, but she had to tell this story and I knew I had to hear it.

'She just said this had gone on long enough, that I was her daughter and I had to allow her back into my life. No apology, no explanation. She didn't even ask about Noah. When I mentioned him, she just said that she would accept 'that boy'.

She paused for a moment, struck by the words she'd spoken. Nothing justifies murder, but I felt sad for Noah.

'So obviously I told her nothing had changed, I

wanted nothing to do with her. And that was the last I heard of it for a while. Until one day earlier this year Noah came home telling me that their new Head Teacher would be a Miss Finch. She'd always used that professional name; it was her mum's maiden name.

'I couldn't believe she did that. I wouldn't let her back in my life, so she became the Head of my son's school? I also heard from Carol she was looking to move to the village. That was so typical of her. She manipulated Tim into becoming Chair of Governors, and then he struck a deal for the school to join her academy chain.'

'Why was she so desperate to be back in touch with you?'

'Who knows? Power, control. She was used to everyone doing what she said and, when they didn't, she had to punish them for it. She did it when I was pregnant with Noah and then again when I wouldn't make up with her.'

I looked at the cartoon seaside images behind her. They looked different now – less fun, less innocent. 'You didn't have to kill her.'

'She crossed a line when she messed with my son. At first it was... well, you know about this, stopping him helping in the school at open evenings and stuff.'

It was true. 'That boy' was to be kept out of

sight and discouraged from helping at all events. I always thought it was her prejudice against his disability.

'But then she tried to stop him going to the sixth form. We had a letter saying his predicted grades weren't high enough and recommended that we looked at East Sussex College. I didn't even tell Noah about it. Then, he told me that a girl called Gracie kept being mean to him. He had no idea it was his own cousin!

'So I went to see Tim. I told him to tell his daughter to leave Noah alone, but more importantly, that his sister had gone too far. He tried to smooth it over, but he was just her puppet; he was so weak.

'Then I had an official letter inviting me in to have a meeting with 'Miss Finch' about Noah. She told me to my face, with Tim sat there too, Noah wouldn't be returning to the sixth form - it wasn't the right post-sixteen placement for a pupil with his needs. She gave me a copy of their admissions policy to show that she was acting within the right guidelines. And then she smiled at me - the most smug, evil, victorious smile I've ever seen.'

She stopped for a moment. 'It was then I knew I would make her pay.'

'You mean you decided to kill her?' The disgust in my voice was apparent.

'Don't you see, Edward? I'm messed up. The way she disowned me, and all the emotional abuse when I was growing up, she made me like this. I know it's not a normal reaction to want to kill someone, let alone go through with it. But it was her fault.'

This was not the kind, down-to-earth woman I'd started to fall for just a couple of days ago. But that was fiction. This was reality.

'And trying to frame Brian? What did he do to deserve that? You were friends with his wife.'

'Edward, someone had to take the blame.' Her face was emotionless as she continued. 'He was always horrible to Noah, why not him?'

'And what about Tim?'

'He definitely deserved to be framed for it. If he hadn't helped her, she'd never have come here.'

'But Emma, you killed him. You took a sixteen-year-old's dad away from her.'

'That wasn't supposed to happen. He caught me planting the keys and threatened me. He was so smug, saying I would pay for killing his sister. I saw the ornament and when he turned away I just reached for it.'

There's never a justification for murder in my eyes, but at least with her Mum there was deep-seated hatred which led to it. Her explanation for killing Tim was just callous, and I made an observation out loud. 'I think it's Miss Marple who said that once someone has committed one murder, they don't shy away from another.'

She sighed and stood up, walking towards the café counter. 'Is that right? What do you think we should do now then, Edward?'

'You don't have the right to take people's lives away, no matter what they've done. It's wrong.'

She walked back towards me. 'I wish I could think like you,' she said sadly. 'You've had your own issues, but you're so kind. That's why I liked you. You're the person I could never have been.'

'Yet straight after our first proper conversation you poisoned Miss Finch's water dispenser.'

'The question is, Edward...' she paused. She had returned to the table, but rather than sitting back down, she stood hovering at her seat. Out of nowhere, she produced a kitchen knife from her apron and pointed it at me. 'What are you going to do about it?'

We looked at each other for what seemed like an eternity; an insane, deadly version of one of those blinking challenges. I could feel my anxiety rising, feeling the danger acutely for the first time. It was my own fault; I'd read so many novels where the detective puts themselves in danger by confronting the murderer alone. But I didn't think of it like that – yesterday, Emma kissed me. Maybe I'd let my emotions get the better of me. I shouldn't have got myself in this situation.

Then, the moment was broken, but not in a way either of us expected. A key turned, and the door opened.

'Mum put the knife down. You can't kill Mr Crisp.'

Emma, with madness in her eyes, turned to her son. 'It's okay Noah, we're just playing a game.' Her eyes darted from him back to me, thrown off track by this latest development.

'Mum, it's okay. I've been standing at the door. I know everything.' He suddenly realised he hadn't greeted me. 'Hello Mr Crisp, are you okay?'

'I've been better, Noah.'

'I heard you say how you worked everything out. I knew you'd solve it, Sir.'

This was madness. He sounded like he was talking about the plot of an Agatha Christie novel, not his own mum's murder spree.

'Noah, wait for me at home, you're not involved in this.' She still had the knife pointed at me, but her hand trembled.

'I am involved, Mum,' he replied. He glanced behind him in the doorway he was still standing in. 'I'm sorry but you're the killer, and in murder mysteries the killer has to be punished.'

He looked again over his shoulder, and DI Appleby appeared. 'Put the knife down, Emma.'

She hesitated, and I could tell she didn't know what to do. But, in a flash, DC Gillespie, PC Wood and another male officer with ginger hair stormed past me and grabbed her.

Appleby stepped forward. 'Emma Oxley, you are under arrest on suspicion of the murders of Anne Finch and Tim Hunt. You do not have to say anything, but it may harm your defence if you do not mention when questioned something which you later rely on in court. Anything you do say may be given in evidence.'

Noah stood calmly, not showing any emotion.

'I love you, Noah,' Emma screamed as the officers led her out.

'I know you do, Mum. But you're the murderer. The police need to take you away now.'

41

'I can't believe you worked out it was Noah's mum. I thought it could only be Noah himself after I found his novel.'

We were in the pub later that evening and I was explaining everything. As well as Patrick and Kat, my brother and Dylan were sat with us and my parents were hovering in the background. Even though it was a Monday afternoon, Dad had decided the occasion was special enough to do an impromptu DJ set, playing an array of inappropriate songs like *Devil Woman, Killer Queen, Murder She Wrote* and other numbers themed around the case that my brain has blocked out.

'I still can't believe I had a murderer at my dining table,' my mum said from the bar. 'I thought she would be my daughter-in-law. It makes me shudder just to think about it.'

Kat noticed the expression on my face and nudged me. 'Are you okay?' she whispered. I nodded, in spite of what I felt inside.

'But the main thing is our son worked it out, all by himself,' my dad said, walking over from his DJ desk with his pint in his hand. 'The police didn't have a clue, but our Edward did... to Edward.' He raised his glass.

'To Edward,' everyone repeated, doing the same.

This didn't feel right. 'Thanks everyone, I appreciate it. But two people are dead and it leaves two teenagers without parents.'

'I'm going to ring social services about both Noah and Gracie tomorrow,' Kat said. 'See if I can find out what will happen to them. Hopefully, they'll get hold of Gracie's mum.'

'Noah has no one though, does he?' Patrick asked.

'Actually, while we're talking about that,' my mum started in a way that made it clear she was about to make an announcement. She glanced over and I nodded – this was something she'd discussed with me earlier. 'Casper and I had a chat, then we talked to a social worker ourselves. We want to help Noah so we've asked if we can take him in for the short term while we apply for foster carer status. It sounds complicated - something about ships.'

'It must be kinship care,' Kat suggested.

'That's the one!' Mum replied.

'Yes, you'll have informal kinship care at first, where a friend or family member look after the child, while you apply for kinship foster care for the long term.' Kat's knowledge of procedures for young people was excellent as ever; she would make a fantastic Head Teacher.

'You sound exactly like the social worker,' Dad replied. 'It all sounds complicated but we're going to get the ball rolling.'

'Linda, Casper, that's wonderful!' Dylan exclaimed as he jumped up to hug Mum. 'Alfie and I will help as much as we can.'

'Thank you, Dylan,' Mum replied. 'It makes sense, we have that massive flat upstairs and we really need to be sitting back and letting Alfie run the pub more.' I caught a grin from my brother.

Just then the door opened, and the Fletchers appeared. Carol stood behind Brian and ushered him forward first to speak.

'Am I welcome?'

My brother stood up and walked over to him. 'Of course you are,' he said, stretching his hand out for Brian to shake. 'There's been enough ill feeling round here. Let's all move on.'

Carol immediately went to the bar and hugged my mum, and within seconds I could hear them gossiping about everything.

'Are things okay with you two?' I asked Brian quietly, gesturing towards Carol.

'We've overcome more than that in our twenty years,' he replied. 'I don't blame her for thinking I had that ID, it was just the situation. She was still in shock.'

Just then I heard a text come through on my phone. '*Hello mate, come outside the pub a minute?*'

I went out to find Appleby sat on one of the outdoor benches. 'You should have come in,' I said.

'And risk getting slapped again?' He laughed as he said this. 'I just came to tell you she admitted everything. She'll plead guilty, I imagine.'

'Wow, I wasn't sure if she would.'

'Yeah. I tell you something, mate, that Noah kid was brilliant.'

'I can't believe he rang you after hearing us.'

'Yeah, luckily I was just round the corner questioning the Fletchers again.' He laughed. 'I was way off track, wasn't I?'

'I guess you were.'

'You did incredibly, mate. You'd make an amazing detective. Give me a shout if you fancy it.'

I shook my head. 'I'll stick to reading about them. I'll leave it to the professionals in future.'

'Thank you, mate. And, genuinely, I just want

to say one more time I'm so sorry for everything when we were kids.' He put his hand out for me to shake. 'You're a top guy, Edward Crisp.'

'Come inside and have a drink with everyone,' I said in reply. 'I'll protect you from my mum.'

42

It seemed for most people that everything was fine now; they had forgotten quarrels and accusations thrown during the tense days of the investigation.

I didn't know what to feel. Yes, I'd solved the murder and apparently I was the hero of the hour. But what did it mean for me, really?

Alfie, Kat and Patrick all thought it was proof I could achieve anything: that now I should fulfil my dreams. But what even were they? Kat said she wouldn't be happy 'til she was complaining about copies of my own book taking up space in the living room. Could I achieve my old ambition to be a mystery author? I wasn't sure – it didn't feel right to be making decisions like that right now. So, instead, I wrote this account to get things clear in my head.

And maybe I also wrote this to remember Emma. Maybe she would have been the love of my life if she hadn't turned out to be a cold-blooded killer. Who knows? I know the woman I'd liked wasn't real. I haven't allowed myself to think about it too much, but I know I won't let that happen to me again.

One thing I've given a bit of thought to is my old bully. I wouldn't have patched things up with Appleby if it wasn't for Miss Finch's murder. Mum still isn't happy I've forgiven him, but I think life is difficult enough without holding grudges.

And of course, there were two more people whose lives had changed forever because of the murders. I saw them three days later at the school's GCSE results day. Mum and Dad were hopeful about taking in Noah, but he was still with a temporary foster family for now while they tried to sort it out.

Gracie turned up at school first. She looked tired and weary and stood on her own. I saw other students, her friends and peers, glance at her inquisitively, but she ignored them and came over to me.

'I thought you'd want to know Sir, I got 5 As and 5 A*s.'

'That's brilliant, Gracie. Well done.'

'Miss Parker has just spoken to me and said I can start my A Levels, study from home nearer the time then re-join the classes when I'm ready. I'll repeat a year if I have to.'

I already knew this through Kat, but I didn't tell

her that. 'That's brilliant, Gracie.'

'Yeah, and they got hold of my mum too. My dad didn't have a will, and they were technically still married, so my mum gets our house. She's moving into it with me and will help me raise the baby.'

I was pleased to hear his. It seemed like there was some glimmer of hope for Gracie. Just then though, Noah entered the room and walked over to join us. There was an awkward silence for a moment. But Gracie broke it.

'I'm sorry I was so horrible to you.'

'I'm sorry my mum killed your family.'

Gracie laughed at his bluntness. 'Noah, you are a weirdo. But I like it,' she laughed. 'It's okay, we can't help our rubbish relatives... Hey, I guess we are cousins.'

'Second cousins, actually,' Noah replied. 'But I don't think you'll see my mum around so we can be first cousins if you like.'

'I'd like that,' Gracie said. 'Take care, both of you.' She was smiling as she walked off.

Noah and I were left alone. He was with foster parents in the village, but this was the first time I'd seen him since the scene at the café.

'How are you, Noah?'

'I'm good, Sir. I've just got an A, a B and 6 Cs in my GCSEs. Mostly Cs but my A was in English and my B in Literature. And I'm staying here for sixth form.' I already knew this was another situation Kat had put right.

'How is your foster family?' He didn't know about Mum and Dad's application yet, they were still waiting to confirm their informal kinship care – we didn't want to get his hopes up if it didn't come off.

'They're brilliant. They've got three massive bookshelves filled with books, they must have hundreds and hundreds!'

'That's great!' I said with as much enthusiasm as I could. He'd been through so much and needed something that made him happy.

'Any Agatha Christie in their collection?' I asked.

'No, Sir. But it's okay. I think I'm going to stay away from murder mysteries for a while.'

And as he said this, I thought maybe I would too. But, then again, maybe not.

Get the next Edward Crisp novel, The Snow Day Murders, now:

https://www.amazon.co.uk/dp/B08P9YC3DP

And get a FREE ebook novella, The Mystery Of Jackson King, when you join my mailing list here:

https://bookhip.com/NXRFHV

The Edward Crisp Mysteries:

Who Killed Miss Finch

The Snow Day Murders

The Mystery of Jackson King (novella)

Death In The Closet

Death In A Deckchair (novella)

Ten Green Bottles (Out November 22)

Acknowledgments

I've always dreamed I'd be in the position of writing acknowledgments in the back of my debut novel.

My first thank you goes to my amazing partner, Graeme, who is simply my everything. Anyone who knows him knows how incredible this man is. I wouldn't have got here without everything you do for me.

To Mum and Dad, who have always given me their love and support. As I write this, they will have been married 50 years next month – what amazing role models for how to do relationships. And I can confirm Linda and Casper Crisp are NOT based on them!

Moving on to the book specifically, thank you to my editor and best writing buddy, Ben. If we'd not met I dread to think what state this book would have been in. Your advice, support and humour along the way have been invaluable. Also a shout out to the other fabulous writer friends who have helped in some way along the journey so far – Mairi, Victoria, John, Debbie, Lozzi and Cass.

To my book designer, Marion, for fantastic book covers and a gorgeous village map – you are so talented. To my ad designer, Jonathan, for fantastic graphics for my advertising campaign, all from the goodness of his heart – such a creative and kind man. To Charlie, for helping me name many of the places and characters, including the eponymous Miss Finch. To Kevin, for excellent advice on the fostering process, and to my Science teacher friends, Jon and Katy, for information about poisons! And a massive thank you to my beta readers Jen, Kate, Sue, Steven, Karen, Sarah B, Sarah C and Emma for lovely encouragement and insightful feedback. You're all hired for book 2!

Next, a massive thank you to all of my family, friends and colleagues who have been there for me in so many ways. There's far too many people to name, but the support since I announced this new journey has been incredible and reminded me how many fantastic people I know. Thank you to all friends North and South from the bottom of my heart.

And finally, to my readers and social media supporters, thank you so much for all of the kindness and encouragement, I really hope you've enjoyed reading this.

Made in the USA
Las Vegas, NV
03 February 2023

66710074R00166